A Class of Her Own

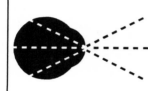

This Large Print Book carries the
Seal of Approval of N.A.V.H.

TEXAS WEDDINGS: BOOK 1

A Class of Her Own

A WOMAN SEEKS LOVE
THAT WILL ENDURE HARDSHIP

Janice A. Thompson

THORNDIKE PRESS
A part of Gale, Cengage Learning

Detroit • New York • San Francisco • New Haven, Conn • Waterville, Maine • London

GALE
CENGAGE Learning

Thorndike Press® Large Print Christian Romance.
The text of this Large Print edition is unabridged.
Other aspects of the book may vary from the original edition.
Set in 16 pt. Plantin.
Printed on permanent paper.

LIBRARY OF CONGRESS CATALOGING-IN-PUBLICATION DATA

Thompson, Janice A.
 A class of her own : a woman seeks love that will endure hardship / by Janice A. Thompson.
   p. cm. — (Texas weddings ; bk. 1) (Thorndike Press large print Christian romance)
 ISBN-13: 978-1-4104-0577-7 (hardcover : alk. paper)
 ISBN-10: 1-4104-0577-X (hardcover : alk. paper)
 1. Widows — Fiction. 2. College teachers — Fiction. 3. Large type books. I. Title.
PS3620.H6824C63 2008
813'.6—dc22   2007049485

Published in 2008 by arrangement with Barbour Publishing, Inc.

Printed in the United States of America
1 2 3 4 5 6 7 12 11 10 09 08

Dear Reader,

Welcome to a collection of faith-based love stories set in the place I know best — south Texas! I was born and raised in this great state and have driven nearly every road mentioned in this tale. And what fun, to have a book titled Texas Weddings. After all, I have four daughters in their twenties, and we've been in wedding-planning mode for the past several years.

A Class of Her Own was my first romance novel, written in 2001. I could relate to Laura Chapman (the heroine) in so many ways. Her desire to go back to college in her mid-to-late forties was a passion I shared. Best of all, I got to plan Laura's "mid-life" wedding. What a blast!

A Chorus of One holds a very special place in my heart. My two oldest daughters got engaged within weeks of each other in 2003, and their weddings were only five months apart in 2004! We were in over our heads as I crafted this story about Jessica Chapman, who longed for a Mediterranean-themed wedding extravaganza. All of my daughters are very musical (and all have been involved in musical theater and/or opera), so placing Jessica's wedding "on the stage" came naturally.

Banking on Love is an "after the wedding" love story. Why did I choose to write a love story about married people? Because I'm always telling my girls, "You're not just planning for a *day;* you're planning for a *life.*" In this tale about a young married couple facing the challenges of post-wedding life, I was able to delve into issues that many contemporary newlyweds deal with and give a few tips about how to keep romance alive along the way!

Happy reading!
Janice Thompson

DEDICATION

This book is dedicated to my mother, Shirley Moseley, an amazing woman of God who, like the heroin in this story, has endured many hardships and come through them all a victor in Christ. In my eyes she will always be in "A Class of Her Own." I love you, Mom.

CHAPTER 1

Laura Chapman stood at the kitchen table, wringing her hands. Something needed to be said, but could she say it? She fought to summon the courage. "I, uh, I'm —"

"What is it, Mom?" nineteen-year-old Jessica asked. "What's wrong?" She continued to clear the dinner dishes from the table, clearly oblivious to her mother's struggle.

"Oh, nothing." Laura attempted to compose herself. This shouldn't be so difficult. She had been through much tougher things than this, especially lately. "See, it's like this, Jessica." She drew a deep breath. "I'm going back to school." *There. No turning back.*

"What did you say?" Jessica looked shocked. The butter knife slipped out of her hand and clattered onto the oak table.

"I said, I'm going back to school." Laura Chapman spoke the words in her most determined voice, though she couldn't seem to hide the tremor. She had wanted to talk to her kids about this for days. Time wouldn't allow her to wait any longer. If she didn't register by tomorrow, there would be no chance — at least not this semester.

"But, Mom," Jess argued, "school?"

"Mom's too cool for school." Fifteen-year-old Kent entered the room with music blasting from the tiny earphones of his MP3 player.

"It's definitely not that." Jessica ignored his obvious attempt at sarcasm. "It's just that you're so, so —"

"So what?" Their eyes met for a showdown of wills.

"Well, you're so —" her daughter stammered, suddenly falling silent.

"Old?" Kent offered, turning up his music to deafen his mother's response.

"Thanks a lot." Laura felt an odd mixture of emotions rise within her as both kids shrugged their response. *I should have expected this.* She tossed her wavy brown hair in defiance, something she might have done at her daughter's age. "You think I'm too old?"

"It's not just that," Jessica argued. "You haven't been to school in, what's it been — nineteen years?"

"Twenty, but I'm sure I can do it." Laura needed a vote of confidence, a confirmation. In the nearly three years since her husband lost his fight with colon cancer, Laura Chapman had lingered on the verge of depression. They were cold, hard years, laced with self-pity and fear. But she refused to give in. She forced herself to get out of bed every morning, dragging herself back and forth to the bookstore where she worked, though it proved to be the toughest thing she had ever done.

When Greg passed away, something in her had died, too. For what seemed like ages, she found herself unable to feel much of anything, unable to dream, to hope. Only in recent days had she begun to come alive again, started to view "tomorrow" as something more than an empty hole to be filled. Surely her children would understand and offer moral support when she most needed it.

"Mom, you just don't understand."

Help me understand. Laura looked into the deep green eyes of her eldest child, her beautiful Jessica — her jewel, her prize. The spitting image of her father, Jessica stood tall and slender, with sleek auburn hair and a light spray of freckles that danced across her cheeks. Her passionate interest in the arts seemed to grow daily, just as Greg's had. She had inherited both his ear for fine

11

music and an eye for the artistic. A fine pianist, Jess always seemed to excel at everything she put her hand to. The grand piano in the living room reminded Laura daily of Greg. He had given it to their precious daughter nearly seven years ago as down payment on her future in the field of music. Now it stood as a reminder that things didn't always work out as planned.

Thankfully, Jessica reconciled herself to studying music at Wainesworth Junior College, a far cry from the university education the anxious teen had craved. She endured it all with little argument — just one in a long list of necessary sacrifices.

Greg would have made sure she received all she needed and more. Laura sighed as she reflected on her husband's great love for their family. A smile instinctively crossed her lips. Just thinking about him could transport her back to better times. Romantic and funny, he had been the perfect mate. There had been a sensitive side to him as well, one that many men did not possess. What amazing memories Laura held of their years together. Their God-given love had run deep. Greg had truly loved her as Christ loved the church, and being his wife had been an honor.

Lord, I miss him so much. No other man

could come close to Greg. He'd given of himself day after day, working hard to provide for their family. He'd made himself available to the children and had been genuinely interested in their wants and needs. He'd planned so much for them, so much more than she could give them.

Her daughter's dancing green eyes proved to be a reminder of his spunk, his tenacity, and his undying love. Jessica was, in every way, Greg's child. And yet, Laura had to admit, her eldest also bore a determination that trickled down from Laura herself — a stubbornness that could only be traced back to her own side of the family.

"What don't I understand?" Laura asked, coming back to life again. Surely her daughter could come up with nothing that she hadn't already considered herself. She had argued the negatives and positives of this decision with herself for several nights as she twisted and turned in the sheets.

"Things aren't like they were when you were in school, Mom. They'll eat you alive in college." Jessica gave her a confident, knowing look, one that could not be ignored.

Kent added his two cents' worth. "Yeah, no kidding."

"Thanks for the vote of confidence."

Laura's oversensitive heart felt the betrayal, but she bore it with a stiff upper lip.

"Anything I can do to help, Mom." Kent shuffled from the room, earphones still in place and music blaring as loudly as ever.

Jess shook her head, obviously unwilling to give up the fight. "Mom, you don't get it. The students are really crude, the professors are even worse, and the workload is a killer. I barely made it last semester myself. You see how it is. I had homework every night last year — hours of it. How would you make it with your job?"

"I can work part-time at the store in the afternoons and evenings, and take morning classes. Besides, if God is for me, and I'm convinced He is . . . who can be against me?"

"I'm not trying to discourage you," her daughter said with a shrug. "I just want you to be practical, that's all. One of us has to be."

"I am very practical," Laura argued. *I've got a solid plan, a good plan. It will work. You'll see.* "Lots of people do this."

"Young people," Jessica argued, lips tight. "Some of them don't make it when they're working and going to school. Remember Bridget Kester? She dropped out of college last spring because she didn't pass any of

14

her classes. She tried to work at the health club and go to school at the same time. College is tough. And she's young. Bridget's my age."

"I know how old she is, Jessica." *Lord, help me keep my temper in check.* "But you're not giving me much credit. It's not like I haven't been to school before." Laura felt her zeal begin to wane.

"Twenty years ago."

"What difference does it make, really? Besides, we're only talking junior college here — not graduate school. I want to get my associate's degree. That's all. I've wanted it for years. I gave up college when you came along, so I never had the chance to —"

"I know, Mom. You've told me a hundred times." Jessica's face twisted slightly, an indication she already carried the guilt of this situation.

Oh, but it was worth every moment just to be with you. Don't you realize that? Haven't I told you enough? Laura carefully reworded her story. "Jessica, I went to college for one year before I married your father. The second — well, the second year was tough. When you're a new bride, setting up house and caring for your husband feels like the most important thing. Marriage can be a little distracting when you're in school." She

15

smiled, remembering those early days — how torn she had been between schoolwork and decorating their first little apartment. Greg had been so proud of her as she chose fabrics and stitched curtains herself. He lovingly helped her hang them, commenting on their beauty. They'd ended up in each other's arms, curtains hanging lopsided from the rod above.

No, there hadn't been much time left for schoolwork. Not then, anyway.

Laura composed herself, continuing on. "At the beginning of the next semester, I found out you were coming. I just couldn't make myself go back. I never could."

But there were no regrets anymore, not about school anyway. Ever since the catalog had come in the mail three weeks ago, Laura had been making her plans, calculating, counting the cost. She would go back to college, and nothing would stop her.

"It's your decision, Mom," Jessica said. "Though I can't help but think it's the wrong one."

Laura shook her head in disbelief. "I love you, Jess. And I want the best for all of us." She turned toward the bedroom, hoping a few minutes alone would put an end to her frustration. She headed to the vanity, where she sat gazing long and hard at her reflection. "I look as tired as I feel." Her weariness would surely increase as she took on the added responsibility of school on top of a job and child rearing. *I need Your strength, Lord.*

Though she fought to remain strong, her faith had weakened over the last three years, truth be told. Still determined to remain close to Him, Laura found herself calling on the Lord more as the months crawled by. Her moments with Him brought genuine comfort. *"I will never leave you nor forsake you."* The familiar scripture ran through her mind. Laura contemplated the words. *Lord, why can't I feel Your presence like I used to?*

Everything felt different now that Greg was gone. He had been such a good spiritual leader — making sure everyone went to church on Sunday, teaching Sunday school, praying with the kids before bed. Lately, she couldn't even seem to get out of bed on Sunday mornings. Her church attendance had wavered over the last few months. It seemed she found an excuse to stay home nearly every week now. *It's just so much easier.* Facing those happy, carefree people proved far too difficult.

Laura ran a brush through her wavy hair, trying to style it in several different ways.

No matter how long she messed with it, the stubborn stuff would only do the same old thing it always had. Her waves cooperated in one direction and only one. She tossed the brush down onto the vanity, ready to admit defeat.

Laura sighed and gazed at the mirror. *Who are you?* she asked the face staring back at her. *I don't really know you anymore. Can you be more than a wife and mother? Can you be a student, too?* An uncomfortable silence lingered in the air.

Reaching over to the bedside table, she picked up the catalog one last time before turning in for the night. In order to obtain the associate's degree she craved, a serious workload lay before her. But, after all she had been through in the last year, it should be a piece of cake. She ran her fingers over the cover, her index finger tracing the letters "WAINESWORTH JUNIOR COLLEGE."

Laura caught a glimpse of her own smile in the mirror. *Nothing to be ashamed of. I have a perfect right to smile. After all, this marks the beginning of a brand-new adventure for me.*

Professor Andrew Dougherty sat at his computer and scrolled through an American

Revolution Web site with renewed zeal. The red, white, and blue background held his interest for a while, though his computer seemed to be dragging tonight. "Too many graphics," he observed.

A history buff, Andrew had much to glean from the Web. With only a few days before school began, he certainly didn't have much time to put together a comprehensive list of applicable sites for his students. He leaned back and rubbed at his eyes. The monitor had really done a number on his vision. The flag's colors were all melting into one rather lackluster shade of gray.

Andrew glanced at the clock on the computer — 2:45 a.m. "No way." Had he really been online that long? Where had the time gone? Too many nights he seemed to sit alone in this chair, wasting the hours. They always managed to slip by like minutes.

Too much time on the Web, old man. Not that he was old, and not that he had much else to do with his time. Still a bachelor at forty-seven, Andrew found himself completely disinterested in things that had appealed to him in his younger years. The Internet had become a friend and companion, filling his evenings with unspoken words and genuine satisfaction. With so many sites to see, chat rooms to visit, and e-mails to send out, he could easily waste a full evening. Most nights were spent online, when he wasn't up to his ears with papers to grade.

Andrew sighed as he thought about his upcoming classes at the college. He leaned back so far in the chair that it almost toppled over. "Careful now!" He nervously typed in the address to a familiar site. He had heard about it through a chat room he frequented — a computerized dating service. "Only $49.95," the header read. "Money-back guarantee." Andrew had, for some time, toyed with the idea of actually filling out the form and entering a credit card number. It was a game he played with himself quite often these days.

But how would he put it? His mind wandered. "Charming middle-aged man —" No. That wouldn't work. Middle-aged would be a definite turnoff. "Charming, academic forty-something." Nah. But what could he say? How could he possibly begin to describe himself? How did people do that?

His fingers began to trip nimbly across the keys — his heart suddenly releasing him to be free with his thoughts. "Ready for love."

Had he really typed that? After fifteen

years of dealing with a broken heart, the time for a change was rapidly approaching. His last relationship had left him wounded in a way that he never wanted to repeat.

Smiling, he continued on. "Romeo is ready to meet his Juliet. Tall . . ." Hmm. A bit of a stretch, perhaps, since he stood at five-ten. "Tanned." He'd be sure to visit a tanning booth as soon as possible. "Blond, wavy hair." "Sandy" would have been a better word, but who cared? And "unruly curls" might have been a more accurate description, but did it really matter? It wasn't like he was actually going to send this thing off, anyway.

Andrew stared at the screen and faced the next question with some scrutiny. Hobbies. They wanted to know what he did for fun. In all honesty, he sat at the computer and browsed the World Wide Web for fun. But that didn't really sound right. "Romantic walks on the beach," he typed with a smile. South Texas beaches were tolerable enough, he supposed — as long as people weren't crammed onto every square inch of them. Besides, that's what ads like these were supposed to say. "Books." That much was true. "And movies." That one wasn't far off either.

There. All done. Andrew's heart pounded

in his ears. His palms grew sweatier with each keystroke. The undeniable had occurred. He had actually completed the form. A first. All he needed to do was pull out that credit card and —

"Wait a minute!" he said, startled. "Just what do you think you're doing?" He quickly closed out the site and turned off the computer with a vengeance. This time he had come too close for comfort.

No need to worry about that. The peace and quiet would end soon enough. Within days, his hours would be filled with the usual hustle and bustle of college students entering and exiting his classroom. He felt his pulse slowing as his mind shifted to the thing he loved most. *American history. A subject I can handle. No great risks there.*

There seemed to be a certain comfort to teaching history at Wainesworth Junior College. So what if his classroom had a revolving door? Students enrolled, came, then left quickly. *Lazy. So many of them just don't know what it means to earn their grades.* So he might be a little tough. There were far worse things a teacher could be accused of. No shame in admitting he made his students work hard. Most lived easy lives — too easy, to his way of thinking. His college professors had been plenty tough on him, preparing him for life. These students needed to be just as prepared. He would give them all a fresh dose of reality.

Laura tossed and turned in bed, trying to sleep. Her excitement wouldn't allow it — at least, not yet. She made out the glowing yellow numbers on the clock: 2:34 a.m. Even if she managed to doze off, she would only get in five hours. *I don't want to run the risk of getting off to a bad start. Not on such an important day.* Laura propped herself up on three pillows, thinking through her class schedule once again.

Her thoughts held her captive, as they so often did these days. Laura had far too much on her mind to sleep. What would she say to Greg, if she had the chance to talk to him? How would she explain her decision about going back to school? She could see his smiling face in front of her, nodding as she explained herself away. His auburn hair shimmered in the afternoon sunlight as he listened intently, and his cheeks held the color of a healthy man.

But she would never talk to Greg again. She would never know how he might have felt about this. As difficult as it might be, she had to begin making her own decisions and sticking with them.

Laura listed the courses in her head again, just to be sure she hadn't forgotten anything. Tomorrow would be a critical day, and she didn't want to risk anything going wrong.

CHAPTER 2

"Excuse me. I wonder if you could direct me to the admissions office." Laura's voice trembled with a mixture of nerves and excitement.

The woman in front of her looked too young for college. *"You think you're getting old when high school students start looking like kids, but you know you're getting old when college students look like kids."* They were Greg's words. She remembered them as clearly as if he had just spoken them.

The girl turned and looked at her curiously. "Up those stairs," she said in a cheery, youthful voice. "Take a left at the first hallway, then follow it all the way to the end. Turn right and go about twenty feet, and then take another right. About three hallways up on the left you turn again. You should see Admissions directly in front of you. There's a bright blue sign just above the door."

Laura couldn't be sure she had absorbed the directions, but she didn't ask the young girl to repeat herself. *This is all so embarrassing, and I feel so out of place.* "Oh, uh, thank you." She found herself distracted by the girl's eyeliner. It was a little too thick on the right eye and smeared a little on the left, a sure sign of puberty. Her skirt was short — a little too short, to Laura's way of thinking.

"Are you registering a son or a daughter?" the girl asked.

How embarrassing. How totally, completely embarrassing. Of course, Laura couldn't blame her for making the assumption. If she had a lick of sense, she would turn around and walk out the door. Instead, Laura shook her head. "I, uh, I'm signing up. I mean I'm going to start classes here." She spoke the words half ashamed, half proud.

"Really?" A sudden look of interest filled the girl's dark brown eyes. "Well, I'm happy to hear it. We need more people your age. I'm Kaycie Conner, head of the English Department."

"What?" Laura tried to decipher this new information, to work it into the equation, but it just didn't seem to compute. *No way.*

"I, uh, I'm Laura Chapman. I'm hoping

to get my associate's degree." Her ability to speak coherently seemed to be slipping away more with each passing moment.

The woman nodded and smiled. "Well, good luck to you. Let me know if there's anything I can do to help."

Laura focused on the young woman as she walked away, unable to speak a word. She began to walk in the direction Ms. Conner had pointed, hoping she'd heard correctly. Her heels clicked against the white tile floor, creating a melancholy echo. The sound seemed to scream out, "Look at me," when she really wanted to disappear into the woodwork. At the end of the hallway, Laura turned and headed up the stairs. Which was it again? Right, left, left, right — or left, right, right, left?

Gratefully, at the top of the stairs, a sign reading ADMISSIONS pointed to the left. She followed a trail of clues until she reached the proper office. Finally. The big blue sign. She breathed a sigh of relief, happy to be at her destination. Not that it made much difference. The line went on forever.

Laura took her place at the end of the line, feeling like a wallflower at a junior high school dance. She half-listened, half-ignored a host of young students as they rambled on and on about this professor and that, griping and cursing. Their language proved to be almost as unforgivable as their attitudes. Jessica had been right about one thing: Teenagers were different these days. Crudeness seemed to be the rule of the day. This amazed yet frightened her.

Off in the corner, a couple stood with their lips locked. *Best to ignore them.* Laura pulled out her catalog for one last excited look at her possibilities. There would be no room for mistakes. She had to get this right. She thumbed through the book, closing it willfully. Her mind drifted ahead, into the vast unknown. *Perhaps someday I'll own my own bookstore. It might be a dream but not an unrealistic one.* She would have not only the courage to achieve it but the wherewithal to accomplish it. She would be bold, confident, daring . . .

"Next."

Laura looked up, shocked to find herself at the front of the line. She gazed into the eyes of a young man, about twenty-one or so. He looked tired and irritable.

"Can I help you, ma'am?" His curt words startled her. "We're about to close."

"Uh, yes. I —"

"Are you here to sign up for classes?" he snapped, glancing down at his watch.

"Yes, I am. Am I too late?"

"That depends. Have you seen a counselor?"

"Yes," Laura spoke quickly. "He gave me this." She pushed a card across the counter and smiled in his direction.

His face softened a little as he read it. "Ah. Working on your degree, huh?"

"Yes." Laura smiled, energized at his sudden interest.

"Don't sweat it, sister," he said. "I'm in the same boat. Most of these kids are."

"Really?" *Not that I'm your sister. And not that I'm a kid.*

"Toughest thing is American History, at least for me. Looks like you're gonna end up with Dougherty. He's the only one still taking students." At that, he let out a whistle.

"What? What's wrong with Dougherty?"

"Harsh guy. He makes his students work twice as hard as the others. But you'll make it. You look pretty tough."

Tough? She suddenly didn't feel very tough.

Andrew entered the empty room with a large cardboard box in hand. He always loved this part of the year — setting up his classroom. He looked forward to it with an unashamed vengeance. American history would soon come alive for a new group of students. He would see to it. On the other hand, if it didn't come alive to them, he would see to a few other things — like extra assignments, for example.

With great excitement, he began pulling maps from the box. One by one, he secured them to the wall. Lovingly, he ran his fingers across the brightly colored map of North America, tracing the path he had taken from Florida, the place of his birth, to Texas, where he found himself planted. It certainly hadn't proven to be the location of his dreams, but at least he could work in the one field that made him happy. Not everyone could say that.

Andrew backed away from the wall, looking at it carefully, curiously. There seemed to be something missing, but he couldn't quite put his finger on it. *Ah yes.* He groped through the box in search of his prized copy of the Declaration of Independence that lay inside.

"There you are," he said with a proud smile. "Thought you could hide from me, eh?"

He unrolled it with great care, reading as he went along. The edges were frayed and the printing worn, but the words still captivated him, kept him locked in their grip — even after all these years. The founding fathers had worked diligently on the vital document so that he could have freedom, so that he could one day live out the American dream. Just the idea brought a rush of patriotic pride.

"Better get a hold of yourself." Andrew shook his head. "People might start to think you've got a screw loose."

Ah, let them talk. Folks already thought he was an oddball, anyway — forty-seven and still single. They had their probing speculations, to be sure, though he did his best to ignore them. Why bore them with the details, anyway? His heartbreak fifteen years ago wasn't any of their business. They didn't need to know the one woman he had ever given his heart to had jilted him.

No, no one at Wainesworth Junior College would ever have to know.

Laura left the crowded college bookstore with five minutes to spare, her arms loaded with textbooks in varying shapes, sizes, and colors. They had to be carried out to the car — which was parked a good half mile away in the farthest parking lot. The weighty stack of books blocked her vision, and her arms ached already.

Laura turned the corner and ran headlong into a tall man with sandy-colored hair. Her books tumbled to the tile floor with a crash, scattering about in every conceivable direction. Her purse flew from her arm and hit him squarely in the belly. He doubled over and let out a groan.

"I'm — I'm so sorry!" Laura dropped to her knees. *I won't look into his eyes. I can't. This is so embarrassing.* "Really, I just wasn't looking where I was going." Her heart beat loudly in her ears. She found herself eyeball-to-eyeball with a man, a nice-looking man, and it scared the living daylights out of her.

"No problem." He reached down to help her pick the books up. "But that purse of yours packs a pretty heavy punch."

Laura groaned loudly. "I'm sorry. I really am."

"You might want to invest in a backpack before classes start next week," he said with a grin. "That's what most of the students carry. You are a student, aren't you?"

Laura looked up at him, grateful for the acknowledgment. "Yes, I am." Frankly, she was so relieved to see someone her own age, she hardly knew what to say. *Hopefully, he's a student, too.* His curly hair was a little unkempt, but not unforgivably so. Their eyes met in an embarrassed glance. The gentleman placed her American History book on top of the pile, looking at her intently.

"Are you taking American History?"

Why is he staring at me? Laura wondered, fighting to balance the stack of books.

"Yes, I just signed up, but I'm not looking forward to it." She shuddered as she remembered what the young man at the registration desk had said.

"Why is that?" The stranger reached to catch the history book as it slid from her grip again.

"Oh," she said, clutching it tighter, "it's not the class. It's the professor."

"Really?" He looked at her curiously. "Who do you have?"

"Dougherty. I hear he's tough. Really tough."

"Tough, huh?"

"Yeah," she said with a sigh. "Hope I'm up for it. What about you?"

"Me?" he said with a look of chagrin. "Me? I'm late for a meeting. Have a nice day." He turned abruptly and walked in the opposite direction.

CHAPTER 3

Laura buzzed around the kitchen in happy anticipation. Once the registration process drew to its logical conclusion, she finally enjoyed a good night's sleep. The world suddenly seemed a much brighter place. *I'm going to make it.* Laura took a sip from her cup of coffee, glancing out the kitchen window. The yard needed mowing, but even that didn't deter her this morning.

Kent, walked in, yawning. "Morning, Mom." He looked groggy. "What's for breakfast?"

"I signed up for classes yesterday," Laura said excitedly. It wasn't exactly "Bacon and eggs," or "Good morning," but it seemed to be the only thing that would come out of her mouth. She didn't even try to disguise her zeal.

"Yeah, Jessica told me," he replied with a shrug. "She's pretty bummed."

Immediately, Laura felt her expression

change. Jessica must really be upset if she took the time to talk to her brother about it. She rarely talked to Kent about anything.

"It's cool, Mom," Kent continued, pulling open a loaf of bread. "You do what you have to do. Don't let her get to you. I know I never do."

"I won't." Laura said the words but didn't really know if she meant them — at least not yet. Truth was, Jessica did get to her. She always got to her.

"When do your classes start?" Kent reached to stick two pieces of bread in the toaster.

"Next Monday." Laura took another sip of her hot coffee, deep in thought.

"Doesn't seem fair," he said, frustrated. "We've already been in school a week."

"I know. But I'm sure you'll have an easier time than I will."

"That's putting it mildly," Jessica said as she entered the room. "What classes did you sign up for, anyway?" She sat at the table and reached for the nearly empty box of cereal.

Ah. So you're speaking to me, eh? Maybe this wouldn't be so bad. "I'm taking Algebra, English, and a fitness class," Laura said. "Oh, and I managed to sign up for American History. That's the one I'm worried about."

"American History?" Jess looked concerned.

"What's wrong, honey?" Her heart began to pound, dreading a confrontation.

"Nothing. At least not yet." There was an undeniable edge to her voice. "Who's your professor?"

"Dougherty."

Jess turned white. "Not the one-fifteen class."

"Well, yes," Laura said. "Why?"

"I already told you, Mother." Her daughter's voice was laced with anger. "I told you I had an American History class at one-fifteen."

"But you said your professor's name was Miller — or something like that. It's not like I planned this. In fact, I was very careful to avoid this situation."

"When I went to sign up, Miller's class was full," Jess explained. "And I got stuck with Dougherty. Trust me, he's the last one on the planet I ever wanted."

"What's wrong with him?" Laura asked, more than a little curious. "Surely he can't be as bad as everyone makes him out to be."

"He works his students to death, and I've already got too many other classes to worry about. But I had made up my mind to get through it somehow. If I had known . . ."

"Neither of us could have known," Laura argued. "I guess it just couldn't be helped. He was the only professor still taking students at that time."

"I know, I know. But can't you take history at another hour?"

"No, I really can't." Laura couldn't possibly adjust her schedule. Everything had been carefully arranged. She needed to be at work by three in the afternoon.

"Mother, you don't understand. I *have* to take an American History class. It's required."

"And you don't seem to understand," Laura countered. "I *have* to take it just like you do. I'm working on my degree, too."

With the shake of her head, Jessica turned and left the room.

Andrew sat at the small, round breakfast table, swallowing a fried egg and two pieces of bacon. His morning routine hadn't changed in decades. He carefully wiped the edges of his mouth, feeling the draw of the computer. *I've probably got just enough time to check my e-mail before heading up to the college.* Andrew hoped to find something special today — a letter from a colleague with important news.

He placed his plate in the dishwasher, realizing it would be several more meals before he had enough dishes in there to actually warrant turning the dumb thing on. Sooner or later, the plate would get washed. Living alone had its benefits. Anything beat a sink full of dirty dishes and toys lining the stairs. That would be awful. Probably.

Using an antibacterial spray, Andrew wiped down the counter meticulously — not just once but twice. He couldn't be too careful. With school starting in a few days, there would be enough germs to battle in the classroom.

He made his way into the small cubbyhole he called an office and turned on his computer. Barely three months old, it flew on with great speed. Andrew enjoyed investing in the latest technology. He had to keep up with the times, especially today. What else did he have to spend his money on, anyway? *It's not like I have a wife and kids to support.*

"Snap out of it," he said aloud, shaking his head. He didn't need a reminder about marriage, at least not yet. He sat in silence as the computer booted up, then raced to sign online. *Today's the day.*

The familiar "You've got mail" rang out, creating a little stir. He scrolled through the pieces of e-mail, mostly junk. No letter. He sat back in the chair, feeling the rejection intensely. Hadn't Joe said he would write back today with news of . . .

Aw, what difference did it make anyway? No woman on the planet would be interested in him, blind date or otherwise. Andrew snapped the computer off, not even bothering to shut it down in the usual fashion. He stared at the black monitor, deep in thought.

Karen. He thought about her every day. She was the first thing to cross his mind in the morning, and the last thing he reflected on at night. His Karen.

Just out of graduate school, Andrew had met Professor Karen Norris at a dinner for incoming staff. Of course, that had been light-years ago, in a completely different state. But he had noticed her the minute she walked in the room — dark hair, slim figure, deep brown eyes. Perfect in every way. Karen.

Well, almost every way. They had connected on more than an intellectual level. He fell head over heels for her, and she had for him — at least, that's the way it looked and felt at the time. Their years together escalated into plans for matrimony, a state he had grown to desire. They planned, plotted, and strategized. The future looked like a field of endless possibilities.

And then . . .

Andrew pushed himself up from the chair. *I won't play this game today. Thousands of times I've thought about her, and where has it gotten me?*

No. Today the whole world lay at his feet.

Laura threw a load of clothes into the washer and tossed in a cupful of detergent. She missed the mark only slightly — about half of the detergent landed on the washer and the other half in it. "What are you doing?" Scolding herself, she swept her hand across the gritty stuff, brushing it into the machine. She slammed the lid shut, turned the button on, and leaned back against the washer to think.

Lord, this isn't working out like I need it to. Show me what to do, Father. Her mind couldn't seem to release the earlier conversation with Jessica. Going back to school might be impossible. Doing so would humiliate her daughter. That much had been made painfully clear.

The hum of the washer coursed her thoughts along. She had already invested so much money into the venture. She couldn't possibly stop payment on the checks she had written. That would be impractical, and she would end up feeling foolish about the whole thing.

Laura turned to look at the kitchen table, piled high with textbooks. She sighed deeply and then made her way over to them. She had really looked forward to the fitness class, and the English class, too. Algebra would be a challenge, but her determination could see her through that, even if it meant spending extra hours in the math lab. But American History — that presented a completely different problem, one she couldn't seem to find an answer to. Laura ran her fingers over the cover of the American History textbook. A picture of the Liberty Bell adorned the front of the book, pealing out the message of freedom, liberty, and failure.

Was this really all that divided her from Jessica — a crazy American History book? Irritated, Laura tossed it on the floor.

CHAPTER 4

Laura picked up the telephone to call her mother for a heart-to-heart chat. Somehow, with all she had been through in the last few years, she craved her mother's companionship most. Perhaps the fact that her mom had already walked this road ahead of her drew them together.

Laura's own father passed away in his forties, the victim of a massive heart attack. Her mother limped through the grieving process and somehow managed to come through it a stronger woman. She transitioned from victim to victor. Her great faith pulled her through. She'd never let go of the Lord's hand. Her marriage to Buck a few years later led to many happy, comfortable years. Buck was wonderful for her mother. His personality proved to be as refreshing and down-to-earth as his name.

"Mom?"

"Laura? I was hoping you'd call today. I've

just got a few minutes. My quilting club meets in half an hour at the church." Somehow just hearing her mother's voice sent a wave of happiness through her. Her mom reflected such joy — and peace. She always seemed to ride a wave of tranquility. Laura needed that.

"I know, Mom. I just needed someone to talk to for a couple of minutes."

"What's up, Laura?"

She felt the familiar knot in her throat. "I went to the college yesterday." She tried to keep her voice steady.

"Good for you." Her mother's voice rose in pitch. "Just what I wanted to hear. Well, how did it go?"

"Not bad, really." Laura dabbed at her eyes with a tissue. "But I've upset Jessica."

"Jessica?" Her mother's voice changed slightly. "What's wrong with our girl?"

"She doesn't want me to go to school with her, and I'm not so sure it's the right thing anymore."

The silence on the other end startled her. When her mother finally spoke, the voice seemed exceptionally stern. "You mean to tell me you're going to let your nineteen-year-old daughter control your chances for happiness?"

Wow. Quite a comment from a woman who

43

prides herself on her soft, gentle nature.

"I wouldn't go that far, Mom." Laura chose her words with care. "She's had such a hard time since Greg died — in some ways, even harder than Kent. And she's enjoying college so far. I don't want to ruin that experience for her."

"Listen to me, Laura Marie," her mother said, suddenly sounding quite motherly. "Once upon a time I almost let you do the same thing to me, remember?"

Laura did remember, and the memory still carried the guilty sting of a teen who had treated her mother badly. *I was so young then and so selfish. If I had it all to do over again, I would . . .*

"There was a time many years ago when I almost stopped my relationship with your stepfather before it started."

Laura remembered all too well. She had behaved very badly. But Buck hadn't seemed right for her mother — at least not at first. Of course, time proved differently, and the guilt she carried over her childish behavior still plagued her from time to time. *We make mistakes when we're young, but time has a way of teaching us the lessons we need to learn.*

"I had just met Buck," her mother continued, "and he invited me out to dinner. You

44

told me, quite bluntly, if I recall, that if I went out to dinner with him, you would never speak to me again."

The knot in Laura's throat began to grow. "But I didn't mean that, Mom. It was just the grief of losing Daddy speaking." Twinges of guilt gnawed at her again.

"Same with Jessica," her mother said firmly. "Just listen to me. I went on and defied you, taking the risk you wouldn't speak to me. Oh, I knew you would eventually, but I really worried my decision might cause a rift in our relationship. I forged ahead and did what my heart told me to do."

"And it's all worked out for the best, hasn't it, Mom?" Laura knew she spoke the truth. No doubt about that. Buck had turned out to be the best thing that could have ever happened to her mother.

"All for the best," the older woman said confidently. "But not without a lot of prayer on my part. Maybe that's what's missing here, Laura. Have you really prayed about your decision to go back to college?"

"Yes, Mom, I've prayed about it for weeks." *I've asked for direction from the very beginning.*

"How do you feel when you've prayed?"

Laura thought about that a moment before answering. Except for the small jittery moments, she had been comforted by an incredible amount of serenity about the decision. "I've had peace," she said, "until now."

"So what you're telling me is you're going to let Jessica disrupt the one decision that has brought you peace?"

"Well, when you put it that way —" Laura felt a resurgence of energy. She'd been excited by the idea of going back to school from the very beginning. It seemed so right.

It *was* so right. Suddenly everything became very clear. "Mom, you're a miracle worker."

"All mothers are. Just keep your wits about you when Jessica gets her skirts all twisted up in a knot. Don't let her control you. Stop it before it starts. You do what's best for you."

"I love you, Mom." The words were heartfelt, genuine. Laura only hoped someday she might be half as amazing as her own mother.

Andrew yawned and folded the evening paper. Politics — the usual rhetoric. That's all he encountered as he glanced through the pages. "Not much worth reading about." But what else could he do? He could squander a few minutes going over notes for his first lecture on the Vikings' exploration of America, but he'd given that lecture dozens of times before. Nothing new there. What would be new was the much-awaited e-mail from his colleague Joe Morris about the promised blind date. He leaned back against the couch cushions and tried to imagine what she might look like.

Funny, the only the face that flashed before him was that of the woman in the hallway at school — the one with the American History book. Andrew suddenly found himself irritated. *I felt sure she would be a great student, a hard worker. But it looks like she's going to turn out to be just like so many of the others. Lazy.*

"Jess, you're home!" Laura looked into her daughter's eyes. They were red and swollen, along with the tip of her nose — a sure sign something was amiss. "What's wrong?"

"Nothing." Jessica headed toward her room with her focus shifted down toward the floor.

Something was wrong, all right. "Jess, tell me."

"It's nothing, Mom."

"Well, I need to tell you something." Laura heard the quiver in her voice as she spoke. She didn't want to hurt her daughter but had to speak these words.

"What, Mom?"

"I've decided I'm going to go —"

Jessica's bloodshot eyes looked directly into hers.

"I'm going back to school, Jess — even if you don't understand. I have to. It's the hardest thing I've ever done, but it's the right thing for me — for all of us."

Andrew tossed and turned in bed, a Technicolor dream enveloping him. He stood near the door of his car, just about to step inside when a beauty with dark brown hair walked up to him.

"Have you got the time?" she asked, eyes glowing. Her soft, pretty face captivated him. Her hair, tied back with a yellow ribbon, flowed down to her waist.

"I've got nothing but time," he answered, swinging the door open. His voice remained rock-solid, his hands steady.

She looked at him with a smile, and his heart began to beat wildly. She clearly seemed interested in him. He would do his best to impress her. "What've you got in mind?" He tried to look casual.

"I was just thinking . . . ," she said demurely.

"Yes?"

"I was just thinking," she said with a smile, "that if you've got the time — you might want to get that tire checked." She pointed to his left rear tire. Flat. The sound of her laughter echoed through him to the very core of his being. She disappeared into the mist.

Andrew groaned in his sleep, twisting among the covers until they caught him in their embrace.

Laura bowed her head to pray, feeling the weight of the day's decisions slowly lifting. Her heart spoke the words that needed to be voiced. The prayer was deliberate and sweet, not so much a prayer of frustration as one of praise. Funny how much better things suddenly seemed. She hadn't been avoiding the Lord — not really. More like holding Him at arm's length.

I should go back to church on a regular basis. Greg had served as Sunday school teacher for nearly twenty years at their local congregation, and she loved the people, but just the thought of attending sent a shot of pain through her heart. The memories were too fresh, too deep. How could she go from being a wife, seated next to her husband in the pew, to a widow, seated alone?

Everything was different. There would be

no more couples' parties, no more camping trips with friends. Somehow, when Greg passed away, Laura lost far more than just her relationship with him. She lost everything.

CHAPTER 5

With her nerves on edge, Laura entered Room 314. Her first three classes had gone far better than expected, but she genuinely dreaded this one. American History. If it proved to be even half as bad as everyone predicted, she needed to be on the ball before the ball even got rolling.

Laura intentionally arrived early, choosing a desk near the front. She hoped this move might win her a little favor with the slave-driving professor she'd heard so much about. She glanced about the room, surprised at its appeal. *He sure takes a serious interest in the subject matter.* She focused on the Declaration of Independence, which hung on the wall.

A familiar gentleman stood near the door. Laura smiled as she gazed at the fellow with sandy curls who had helped her with her books. For some inexplicable reason, her heart skipped a beat as she saw him. "Hey, it's you!" she said with a smile. "Have you recovered?"

"I've recovered," he said with a polite nod. His answer was cool — a little too cool. Laura waited for him to take a seat nearby, but he did not. He milled about the room, looking at the walls. Other students entered the class, most sitting as close to the back as possible. Laura watched and waited.

Just as the bell rang, Jess entered the classroom. Laura glanced at her wistfully, hoping, at the very least, for a nod or a whispered hello. It never came. She turned her attention to the door once again.

Where is this professor I've heard so much about? What does he look like? Will he really turn out to be as tough as everyone says? Her heart raced with anticipation. Biting her lip, she pulled out a notebook and began to write: AMERICAN HISTORY, AUGUST 26.

The sandy-haired gentleman hadn't yet found a seat. Laura wondered at his boldness, his apparent lack of fear. *Isn't he as worried about Dougherty as the rest of us?* His eyes met hers for a brief moment before he moved toward the blackboard at the front of the room.

"What in the world . . . ?" she whispered.

He began to write in large, concise letters . . . M-R. D-O-U-G-H-E-R-T-Y.

Everything after that became a blur.

Andrew turned to face his class, letting his gaze fall on the middle-aged woman who sat squarely in front. Her skin had drained of its color; her gaze remained fixed to the board. *Good. Let her suffer a little. If her words last week were any indication, she's just as apathetic as the young ones. She probably never had to work a day in her life — just sits at home, watching the soaps and doing her nails. Well, I'll light a fire under her. She's about to find out what real work is all about.*

"My name is Andrew Dougherty." He pointed to the board. "You can call me *Mr. Dougherty.*" The woman's glance shifted to the desk, a clear sign of defeat. *Good. I've got her under my spell.* "I would like to welcome you all to American History — one of the most exciting and difficult classes you'll ever take."

A groan went up from the crowd. This he had grown accustomed to, but it remained part of the drama — and no one could accuse him of not acting his part.

"Oh, I know what you're thinking." He sat on the edge of his desk. "You're thinking, 'I'll transfer out of here and sign up for another class.' "

Another stirring from the troops.

"What sad news I have to convey," he spoke with great drama. "All of the other classes are full. But I promise you this — if you work hard, and if you take great notes, you just might get out of here alive."

Laura managed to keep her emotions in check in the classroom, but once released to the freedom of the hallway, she felt like collapsing. "That class is going to kill me," she said, leaning against the wall.

"I tried to tell you that," Jessica said with a shrug. "But you had your mind made up. Remember?"

All Laura could seem to remember was her run-in with Professor Dougherty in the hall last week. What was it he had said as he reached down to pick up her books? *Are you taking American History?*

"Yes, but I'm not looking forward to it." Had she really put it quite like that?

"Why?" It had been a logical question on his part.

"It's not the course," she remembered saying, *"it's the professor."* Laura shook her head, the memory lingering. If only she could take those words back. She had not only judged him — she had accused him right to his face. *I'm going to reap the*

consequences of that. I can just feel it.

Jessica's voice interrupted her thoughts. "Mom?"

"Yes?"

"You didn't answer me."

"Oh, I'm sorry," Laura turned to look at her daughter. "What did you say?"

"I said, Nathan's going to be picking me up after math and driving me home. Is that all right?"

"Oh, sure, sure —"

"I just don't understand you, Mom." Jessica shook her head. "There are other people in this world who have problems, too. I have my piano auditions tomorrow and I'm scared to death. Did you remember that?"

Laura shook her head in shame. As hard as this was, it was just as hard on Jessica.

Father, help me to concentrate. I need to stay focused!

"I'll talk to you later."

Laura watched as she headed off to another class. Her gaze remained on Jessica, but her mind drifted elsewhere. Frustrated, she turned toward the car. She had only taken a step when she ran directly into someone, her books taking another tumble onto the floor.

"Oh, I'm so sorry," she said, looking up

apologetically at the gentleman. "I . . ."

Could things possibly get any worse than this?

Andrew chuckled all the way to the cafeteria. He had won round one in the great contest he had started with this woman. He could hardly wait for round two. If she survived that, perhaps he would reward her with a pop quiz over chapter one next week. He entered the crowded lunchroom and looked around for a place to sit. Nothing. He made his way up to the counter to order, fighting to get through the mob of teenagers.

"What'll it be, Professor Dougherty?" A plump, dark-haired woman with a friendly face and welcoming voice called out to him from across the counter.

"Well, if it isn't Regina Torres, the best cook in all of Houston," he responded with a playful smile.

"It's Regina Leal now," she said, showing him her wedding ring. "Remember?"

He remembered. "I'm just giving you a hard time. So, how was the wedding?"

"Amazing. But you weren't there! Why didn't you come? I sent you an invitation."

Andrew didn't answer. He had no excuse. It wasn't that he didn't like Regina. Few people at the college treated him with such generosity and kindness. She always made the lunchroom a brighter place with her broad smile and cheery greetings. Her good humor warmed him on days when the cold shoulder from his students left him chilled. No, it had nothing to do with Regina. It was just that the idea of going to a wedding conjured up too many memories of days gone by. It would have been too difficult, far too difficult.

Better to change the subject. "You're back at Wainesworth. I didn't think you'd be working this year."

"Who, me? Leave this place? I could never leave."

"I thought you said that new husband of yours was going to take you off on a cruise or a six-month vacation or something like that."

She shrugged. "Aw, come on, Mr. Dougherty. You know better than that. He works for the cable company. We won't be seeing any European vacations for a long, long time."

Her broad smile cheered him, as always. "Why aren't all women as wonderful as you are?" For whatever reason, his mind shifted to Laura Chapman.

"I guess when the good Lord made me, He broke the mold," she said. "What sort of woman trouble are you having, Professor?"

"Trouble?" he stammered. "No trouble. It's just that most of the women I meet are so . . . so . . ." He wasn't sure what they were.

"It's the women, eh?" Regina said. "Couldn't be the problem's on the other end?"

"I'll have a root beer and a bag of pretzels," he said curtly, reaching for his wallet.

"Great combination. What did you do — skip lunch again today?"

He shrugged. "Yeah. I didn't have time between classes — not today, anyway. Talk about swamped."

"You better take care of yourself," she said. "Stay in good shape for that wife we're gonna snag for you this year."

"I beg your pardon?" He looked at her curiously.

"I'm just saying — with the two of us working together . . ."

"Regina, my love life is none of your business."

"What love life?" she asked as she tossed the bag of pretzels at him. "When was the last time you were on a date?"

"For your information, I'm about to go out on a date."

"Today?"

"No," he said, shaking his head. "But soon."

"With who?"

"A girl named Judy. My friend Joe is fixing me up with her." His heart raced, just thinking about her. *She's the one. I just know it.* After all of these years, it would be so amazing to walk headlong into a romantic relationship. *If anyone deserves it, I do.*

"What's wrong with her?" Regina asked, lips pursed.

"What do you mean?"

"I mean, if she has to be fixed up on a blind date . . ." Regina's eyes reflected her thoughts on the matter.

"There's nothing wrong with her, just like there's nothing wrong with me. Not everyone is blissfully in love like you are. So just let me have my date, and I'll report back to you when it's over. Who knows? She just might be Ms. Right."

"Well, hallelujah to that!" Regina said triumphantly. "Maybe I won't have to play matchmaker after all."

"Matchmaker?"

"I had my mind made up I would find you the perfect wife this year. It was sort of a challenge — almost made coming back worthwhile."

"Very funny."

Her face suddenly took on a serious expression. "Don't you worry, Mr. Dougherty. I've got my eyes wide open. I'll let you know when I meet the girl of your dreams."

"Gee, thanks, Regina." He popped open the root beer. "Keep me posted. I'm on pins and needles."

He turned to leave, feeling a little better about his life. As usual, she had managed to put a smile on his face. There were a few nice women in the world, after all.

Laura opened the car door, deep in thought. How could her day have ended this way? Just when she had to face a full afternoon of work, she had *him* on her mind. Professor Andrew Dougherty. He had proven to be every bit as tough as people said he would be.

No — worse. He had given the class two chapters to read for homework, along with a work sheet and a biography on Christopher Columbus. *How am I going to get all of this done and still have time to work at the store? Lord, I'm going to need more help than I thought.*

Laura climbed into the car and pulled out of the familiar parking lot. Try as she might, she could not stop thinking about what had happened in the hallway. She did her best to forget it, but how could she?

Lost in her thoughts, she drove to the Bookstop, hoping to make it in time for her shift. How could she possibly handle all of this — classes in the morning, working the afternoon? "I must be crazy." She drove on in absolute silence, her thoughts overwhelming her. By the time she arrived at the store, exhaustion had completely consumed her.

Laura fretted and fumed as the hours rolled by at the bookstore. She found herself pacing around, frustration growing. She couldn't focus on her work because of Professor Dougherty. She could see him now with his cocky expression, walking toward the board, spelling out his name: D-O-U-G-H-E-R-T-Y . . . very slowly, for effect. His cool eyes had stared into hers as he turned back toward the class. His motives were unmistakable. *Well, I won't let him interfere with my work here. I can't. I need this job too badly.*

"Excuse me?" An elderly woman spoke, interrupting her thoughts. She looked a little lost.

"Yes?" Laura yanked herself out of the daydream to respond.

"Could you please tell me where I can find the biographies? I just love to read about people's lives."

Biographies. *Reminds me — I need to look through some books for information on Columbus.* "Sure," Laura said. "We have a great biography department. Just follow me." She wound her way through fiction and around the children's area to the nonfiction books. *Dougherty would really love it here in this section.* There were biographies galore from his precious American history. She could just see the excitement on his face.

"Oh, thank you, sweetie," the older lady said with a smile. "Just what the doctor ordered. You know, you can learn a lot about a person from one of these books. It always fascinates me to know what makes folks tick — what makes them happy, sad, angry . . ." She rambled on and on, but Laura stopped listening at some point. *There's no way he can expect us to get through two chapters, complete a work sheet, and write a biography in two days. That's ridiculous.* She realized exactly what must be done.

He gave us his number in class, said to call if we had any problems. Well, this is a problem. I'm going to call Mr. Dougherty and see if there's some way to ease the workload.

Andrew buzzed around his apartment in happy anticipation. The long-awaited phone call from Joe had just come in. His blind date, Judy, would be waiting at The Happy Oyster on Highway 290 and Mangum Road. He had just enough time to get there if nothing went wrong. He slipped on a navy shirt, accidentally tearing a button off as his anxious fingers fumbled with it.

"Oh, man!" He pulled the shirt off and reached for another — a gray-and-white stripe. It wouldn't look great with his dark blue sweater vest, but what did it matter, really? *If she's really interested in me, clothing won't be an issue, anyway.* Andrew pulled on the vest, followed by the jacket. *There. Nearly ready.*

He glanced in the mirror for one last look at his hair. *Curly. Too curly.* He rubbed a little hair gel between his palms and spread it all around. No change, but nothing could be done about that. Andrew sprayed on some cologne with a smile. *I'm going all out for this one.* She would be worth it. He could just feel it.

He grabbed his car keys and raced toward the door, double-checking to make sure he hadn't forgotten anything. Just as his hand hit the doorknob, the telephone rang.

"Forget it." He glanced back. "Let the machine get it." But something in him wouldn't allow that. Could be Joe with a change of plans. Or maybe, just maybe, it was Judy, herself. Andrew dropped his jacket on the bench in the front hall and reached over to grab the receiver.

"Hello?"

Nothing could have prepared him for the voice on the other end of the phone.

"Mr. Dougherty?" The woman stressed his name the way he had so carefully spelled it on the board.

"This is he. With whom am I speaking?"

"Laura Chapman," she said. "C-H-A-P-M-A-N."

"Very funny." He couldn't help but chuckle. "What can I do for you, Ms. Chapman?"

"I'm just calling to make sure I got the homework assignment right. Did you really say chapters one and two, along with the work sheet you handed out?"

"That's right. And don't forget —"

"The biography." They spoke in unison.

"That just seems like a lot of work for two days," she argued. "It's just . . ."

"Just what, Ms. Chapman?"

"Well, I thought maybe I had misunderstood. It just seemed like a lot, that's all."

"Look, Ms. Chapman . . ." Exasperation kicked in. "I know your type. You come into a class like this expecting to breeze through, then reality slaps you in the face. Am I right?"

"Well, actually —"

"Why don't you do us both a favor and drop my class while you can still get a refund? It's obvious this is going to be too much for you." Where the words came from, he had no idea.

"Too much for me?" A renewed zeal seemed to take hold of her. "Who said that?"

"You've done everything but say it. I'm a firm believer in excellence, Ms. Chapman."

"So am I," she echoed. "In fact, you just wait and see, Mr. Dougherty. I'm going to be the best student you ever had."

He laughed out loud.

"I'm not kidding!" she hollered, then abruptly hung up.

Andrew doubled over with laughter. *How delicious!* He dropped down onto the couch, trying to calm himself. He began to picture in his mind the infamous Ms. Chapman — what she must have looked like as she spoke with such energy. What a scene she must have created. A smile crossed his lips as he remembered their first encounter. This woman seemed destined to make him a little crazy.

But wait. Another woman waited for him now. Andrew glanced down at his watch and groaned. He would be late, even if he drove like a maniac. Once again, Ms. Chapman had run him down, though she didn't even know it.

Laura shook violently as she placed the phone back on the hook, but she felt some sense of satisfaction. "I guess I told him!" She forced back a laugh. "Let's just wait and see who he thinks he's messing with." Returning to her work, she found herself energized by an undeniable surge of excitement and hope.

Of course, she had made a rather hefty promise. *"I'm going to be the best student you ever had."* She would keep that promise if it took her all day and all night to do so. What did losing a little sleep mean, anyway — as long as she accomplished her goal?

CHAPTER 6

"Put your books away, and take out a piece of notebook paper and a pen." Andrew spoke the words with a sense of sheer delight. The gaze of every history student locked firmly on him. "We're going to have a pop quiz."

A groan rose from among them. One student in particular held his gaze. Her eyes were unmistakably laced with frustration, but they refused to concede.

"Ms. Chapman," he said, feeling a bit heady, "I noticed from your records that your maiden name is Eriksson." She nodded as he continued. "Our quiz today will cover the journeys of the Viking, Leif Eriksson. No doubt a relative of yours — a great-grandfather, perhaps?" He couldn't resist the temptation, though he regretted the words almost as soon as he spoke them.

The roar of laughter that went up from the class convinced him he had accomplished his goal — humiliating her in front of the group. Doing so suddenly didn't feel very kind, but what could he do now?

With the coolness of a cucumber, she replied, "An uncle."

Her response startled him a little. The class erupted, their laughter suddenly focused on him. His ears began to burn, as they always did when turning red.

"This quiz will be worth ten percent of your overall grade," he announced. "You can leave as soon as you've completed it." The students began to murmur, and rightfully so. *So I'm a little irrational. So what?* Laura Chapman had judged him, slam-dunked him, and all but ruined his date the other night. She wasn't going to humiliate him in front of his students. He wouldn't allow it.

Laura struggled through the pop quiz, amazed at the unfairness of the questions. *"What were the names of Eriksson's children?"* Were they even mentioned in the book?

"Larry, Mo, and Curly," she wrote, lifting her pen with a dramatic flair. If she couldn't beat the professor at his own game, she could surely join him in the lunacy of it all.

The pen slipped from her hand, rolling halfway down the aisle before it stopped.

She felt Mr. Dougherty's gaze on her as she crept down the aisle to pick it up.

"Having a problem, Ms. Chapman?"

She glared her response and sat back in her seat, her hands still shaking with anger. She looked down at the pen, noticing ink all over her fingers. "Great." She made her way up the aisle to his desk.

"Can I help you?" he asked, his eyes peering directly into hers.

"My pen broke. Do you have one I could borrow?"

"Certainly." He reached into his top drawer for a black ink pen. "Don't forget to give it back after class."

Laura gripped the pen as she turned and headed back to her seat. She would overcome this — all of this — if it was the last thing she ever did. She sat with a defiant thud and did her best to focus on the paper once again. Question number two seemed worse than the first one. Number three didn't look much better. She took a deep breath, beginning to write. She would give this an honest effort, regardless.

One by one, the class began to empty. Out of the corner of her eye, she could see students marching back and forth to Dougherty's desk to place their papers in the appropriate basket. Each one left with a sigh. As she passed by, Jessica cast her mother an accusing glare.

Laura sat scribbling, marking through, scribbling, marking through. She had read the chapters. Several times, in fact. It was just that these questions were so poorly worded.

She looked up to discover the professor's eyes clearly focused on hers, an undeniable look of satisfaction on his face. *You're insufferable. Nothing like Greg.*

Wait a minute. Where did that come from? Snap out of it. The pen slipped from her fingers once again, hitting the desk and bouncing off to the floor below. It rolled all the way down the aisle, landing just in front of Dougherty's feet. Laura's head dropped to the desk instinctively. *This is partly my fault, Father! I've let my anger overwhelm me. Help me. . . .*

There were still two unanswered questions on the quiz. She couldn't possibly complete them without getting up for the pen. She stood, making her way up the aisle one final time.

"Time's up," Professor Dougherty said sharply.

Andrew spoke the words with satisfaction. Laura Chapman had already distracted him enough. Thanks to her, his date last night had been a complete fiasco. He arrived at the restaurant fifteen minutes late, much to his own chagrin. Judy, it turned out, wasn't a very patient sort. She wasn't a very intelligent sort, either. She had the looks, no questioning that — a redhead with the appearance of a model but few brains to match. A trip to the dentist would surely have been more pleasant. She spent most of the night whining about everything from his tardiness to the nail fungus under her phony red fingernails. It nauseated him.

Andrew looked again at Laura Chapman as she made her way to the front of the class. She didn't have Judy's figure, and her haircut couldn't compete, but it always seemed to catch his eye. Still . . .

Wait a minute, man. What are you doing?

He forced his attentions back to the where they should be, pushing thoughts of women behind him. They simply weren't worth the trouble.

His eyes met Laura's as she dropped the paper onto his desk. He had clearly upset her, but that had been his intention, after all.

Right?

She left the class in a huff, pulling the door shut behind her. He observed the color in her cheeks as she gave him one last frustrated look.

Andrew glanced through the papers quickly, looking for her quiz. With great satisfaction, he skimmed the page. "That's wrong." He struck a red line through her first answer. "And that's wrong." He added more red to the page.

A sea of crimson ink covered the page before he had finished. Andrew leaned back in his chair and smiled, content. Justified, even. She'd gotten exactly what she deserved.

"Well, Ms. Chapman," he spoke aloud to an empty room. "Looks like you didn't do very well on your first American History quiz. But don't worry — you'll have plenty of others in the weeks ahead. I'll make sure of that."

He gathered up the stack of papers from his desk and prepared to leave. He had one last stop to make — the lunchroom. He hadn't eaten all day. Again.

Andrew made his way across the crowded campus to the familiar hub at the center. Teenagers and twenty-somethings surrounded him on every side. He felt his age more acutely than ever in this place. He worked through the maze of kids to the lunchroom inside, where a familiar face greeted him.

"So," Regina said as he approached the counter, "how was your — uh, your 'date'?"

"My date?" He tried to act innocent.

"Yeah," she reminded him. "Remember? You said something about a girl named Judy. How did that work out?"

"Oh, well, you know," he mumbled, looking past Regina at the food choices. "I'll have some cheese curls and a bag of those oatmeal cookies — and a chocolate milk."

"Are you sure about that?" she asked, looking at his midsection. "We're never gonna get you a wife if you keep eating like this."

"Regina," he said with tightened lips, "I told you, I don't need any help. I'm perfectly capable of —"

"Sure you are, sure you are." She collected his food and placed it on the counter. A silence fell between them, lingering in the air for a moment before Regina finally broke it. "By the way, I heard about that pop quiz you gave today." She let out a long whistle.

"What? What did you hear?"

"A killer. That's what I heard."

"Who said that?" he asked, growing angry.

"Who didn't?" came her swift reply. "It's all over campus. You're a legend, Mr. Dougherty. You know that. But they're saying this one really took the cake."

He shrugged. "It wasn't so bad."

"Well, all I'm saying," she leaned toward him, whispering, "is it sounds like you're mighty frustrated with something and taking it out on these poor kids. Why don't you give them a break and let me help you find a wife?"

"The last thing on earth I need," Andrew said forcefully, "is a wife. I'm perfectly happy with me, myself, and I."

"Laura, it's not that I'm complaining," her boss, Madeline, spoke with what appeared to be some hesitancy. "It's just that a couple of our customers have asked about you — wondering if you were okay."

"What do you mean?" Laura looked into the worried gray eyes of her boss. Madeline wasn't the type to mince words. All business, she prided herself on running the bookstore like a well-oiled machine. This showed in the way she dressed, the way she spoke, even in the way she wore her hair. Never married, Madeline couldn't begin to understand the issues of balancing a home and career.

"Well, they seem to think you're a little . . . distracted."

The understatement of the century, Laura

had to admit. She had been here only in body. Her mind and her emotions had been divided between her children and her classes. Factor American History into the equation and, well — there just wasn't a lot left to bring into the workplace.

"I'm sorry, Madeline." She felt the weight of her words as she spoke. "I've been distracted. I know it. But it's only because I'm trying to get used to my schedule, and I've had a little bit of trouble at school. I can handle this. I really can." She sounded like a kid, trying to convince herself.

"What sort of trouble?"

Laura shrugged, not wanting to get into it. "It's really nothing. Nothing I can't handle, anyway. Everything is going to be fine. Just give me awhile, okay?"

"Oh, speaking of trouble," Madeline interjected, "I hate to be the bearer of bad news, but you had a call from Kent's school just before you got here."

"Kent's school?" Laura asked nervously. "What did they want?" *Lord, keep him safe!*

"He's fine. Something about an incident on the bus."

Laura felt the usual twisting in her chest. Her son had spent much of last year in trouble at the junior high. He really seemed to be slipping since Greg's death. But they had talked about it — at great length — just weeks ago. He had promised this year would be different. They had both hoped for a fresh start. Surely he wouldn't blow it this quickly.

"What sort of incident?"

Madeline shrugged. "I told them you'd call as soon as you got in, but you're already late. Make it a quick call."

"I'm sorry." Laura walked behind the counter and picked up the phone, thumbing through her pocketbook for the tiny phone book she always carried. She located the number for the high school and began to dial.

"Carter High School," a cheery voice rang out on the other end.

"I need to find out about my son. I understand he was involved in some sort of an incident on the bus this morning."

"Ah. You must be Mrs. Chapman." Laura's heart sank instantly. "We've been trying to reach you for hours. Can you come up to the school?"

"I just got to work," she said, "and I can't leave."

"It won't take long, Mrs. Chapman, and we really need to talk to you."

"Where is Kent?" She asked the question carefully, dreading the woman's answer.

"He's here in the office, sitting across from me as we speak."

"You mean he's been there all day?"

"Yes."

"I'll be right there." Laura spoke the words, hoping that Madeline would understand. She hung up the phone, heart racing.

"Please let her understand," she whispered the prayer on near-silent lips, then turned, facing her boss.

"They need me to come to the school."

"Now?"

"It's some sort of emergency; at least that's what they said."

"How long will you be?"

"I don't know," Laura whispered beyond the growing lump in her throat. "But I'll come back just as quickly as I can. I promise."

Madeline sighed. "Do the best you can." She shifted her attention to a waiting customer.

Laura turned at once and headed for the door.

CHAPTER 7

Laura sat in the courtyard of the college, battling with her emotions. *September 28. Our anniversary. Today would have made twenty-two years.* She wiped away a tear and reached for her American History book. Distracting herself was the best thing. She could get through this. She thumbed through the text frantically, looking for the right chapter. *I've got Dougherty completely figured out. At least I think I do. I can predict there will, without any question or doubt, be another pop quiz today.* His demeanor in the last class left no uncertainty in her mind.

Staying focused seemed difficult these days. Problems at home escalated daily, causing Laura to be even more distracted than before. She suffered from lack of sleep. Night after sleepless night, she promised herself things would be different, but nothing appeared to be changing. She managed to stay awake reading, studying, writing, or worrying.

Things with the kids weren't much better. Jessica remained in a foul mood much of the time, and Kent had been suspended from school for three days because of his fighting incident on the bus. *When Greg was here, things were so different, so much better — in so many ways.* Kent had always been close to his dad, but now . . .

Now everything felt different. Her son grew angrier with each passing day, and it showed in a variety of ways. Looked like they were in for a rough year.

She needed to remain focused on school things. Despite all of her gloating, Laura's grades were slipping dramatically in American History. A sixty-two on the first quiz set the ball in motion. She hadn't done much better on last week's paper. Her best hope lay in the essay she would turn in today on the Declaration of Independence. She'd spent a great deal of time on it. Of course, Dougherty would find plenty wrong with it. He always did.

Why this particular professor had singled her out remained a mystery to Laura. Surely he couldn't still be holding a grudge after all of this time. There must be something more. But what? Did he hate women in particular, or just her?

79

Sighing deeply, Laura closed the book. Studying seemed to be pointless. His pop quizzes defied logic, anyway. She made her way toward the class, wondering about Jessica. How would her daughter treat her today? Would it be the cold shoulder, or a friendly hello?

Will things be like this forever, Lord?

Somehow, in the midst of the battle, it seemed they would.

Andrew watched Laura Chapman carefully as she entered the room. His disappointment in her had diminished greatly over the past month, replaced with a growing amazement at her tenacity. He hadn't shown that, of course. Andrew looked forward to this class on Tuesdays and Thursdays above all others. All of these changing emotions perplexed him, but not overwhelmingly so. On the surface, she seemed just like any other woman.

Or did she? He looked at her with curiosity. Today she wore a pair of jeans and a soft blue sweater — quite a sight for his sore eyes. Her hair had a shimmer that held him captivated. *She's really very pretty. And maybe she's not as apathetic as I made her out to be. She seems to be trying.*

He quickly changed gears, hoping not to

attract her attention. "Class, please turn in your essays on the Declaration of Independence." He watched as she rose, stepping into the aisle with paper in hand. His gaze never left her. She carried herself with grace. Andrew hadn't yet figured out her story. Was she divorced, widowed? No wedding ring adorned her left hand, and yet she had a daughter, Jessica.

Ms. Chapman placed her paper on the desk — typed, double-spaced — just as he had requested. She certainly seemed to be doing everything in her power to conform. Perhaps the time had come to declare a peace treaty. Enough damage had been done. Clearly she struggled, not just in this class, but with deeper issues. Her eyes were often weary, and her shoulders down. He would change that. He would be a better man. He would step up to the plate.

"Ladies and gentlemen," he said to the class, "today we're going to have an open discussion on the Declaration of Independence. Whom did the authors intend to include? Whom did they exclude? How do you feel about the men who signed, etc.?"

The class erupted into a lively debate — touching on everything from the lives of the men who had framed the document to those excluded from the rights of the Declaration because of the issue of slavery. He kept a careful eye on Ms. Chapman, who never stirred once during the entire discussion. She seemed frozen in place. Finally, when he dismissed the class and the other students left, he approached her. "You were unusually quiet today, Ms. Chapman."

She shrugged her response, but he noticed the frustration in her eyes.

"Nothing to add to the conversation?"

"I just think one subject was overlooked today." She offered up a shrug. "Maybe I should've mentioned it."

"What's that?"

"Well, what about a woman's right to independence — and, in particular, her right to vote? No one even touched on that subject."

"Could you elaborate?"

"I mean, for all the good it did, the Declaration of Independence still didn't provide for the women of those original thirteen states. It excluded them, didn't it?"

"Well, to some extent, perhaps," he said frankly. "But women were viewed differently in those days." *Things are about to get touchy. I can feel it.*

"How so?"

"Well," he said hesitantly, "they were viewed much more as . . ." How could he put this? "They were viewed more as possessions than as thinking people. When a man took a wife, she became his property."

Laura had taken to staring, her jaw hanging open in surprise. "Well, thank God that has changed."

"Yes. Thank God." He paused and then added, "I think that women are completely entitled to their right to vote, as are all American citizens of voting age." He did. No question about that.

"But . . ." Laura looked at him intently.

He chose his words quite carefully. "Well, it's just that some of the women I know aren't exactly nuclear physicists, if you get my drift." Visions of his blind date danced in front of his eyes. Judy's nail fungus had been far more important to her than political matters, that was for sure. Of course, she wasn't like many of the woman he had known, so he couldn't judge them all by the way she'd acted.

"You mean, 'men are smarter than women,' " Laura argued.

Andrew noticed how pale her face had become. It intrigued him but worried him as well. He certainly didn't want to create an even larger rift between the two of them. "Well, no," he stammered, trying to make the best of this. "We're not all smarter . . ."

"All?" Her eyes began to sparkle with anger. Had he said something wrong? No. Every word he had spoken could be backed up with intelligent and accurate statistics.

"Men, as a rule, have a higher intelligence quotient than women," he argued, "but that's because we've been privy to a history of learning, whereas women have only been allowed full access to all of the academic opportunities this country has to offer for a short time. We've got several hundred years of university education under our belts." *There. That should satisfy her.*

Apparently not. She stared at him in silence — deafening silence.

"What I mean to say," he stammered, "is that you — I mean, *women,* haven't had the same access to a college education. You've missed out on many years of possibility." Could he get any plainer than that?

"Are you really saying what I think you're saying? You honestly believe men are smarter than women?"

Her words were heated, and they stirred something in him. She didn't seem to understand where he was coming from. Her stubbornness wouldn't allow it.

"That's not what I . . ." he tried to interject another explanation. He found himself completely frustrated with the direction of the conversation. *How can I turn this around?*

"All you have to do is look around you, Ms. Chapman. You'll find a good many women here at Wainesworth your age but not many men. I'm sure Jessica's father, if he didn't have his degree yet, would head to a major university to obtain his bachelor's or master's. That's true of most men. But you're going to a junior college. See what I mean?" He smiled in her direction.

"I think it's time for me to go," she said, turning to leave the room. Her eyes widened with his last comment, a sure sign she had misunderstood his words. Laura disappeared down the hallway, never looking back. Andrew sprinted after her. He needed to say something to her — obviously something more carefully thought-out than his last statement.

"Ms. Chapman," he called out her name, but she kept walking. "Ms. Chapman." Nothing. "Laura!"

At this, she turned and looked at him, ashen-faced. "There is one thing you should know, Mr. Dougherty, one very important thing."

"What?"

"My husband died nearly three years ago after a terrible battle with cancer. Does that answer your question about why I'm struggling? He never cared if I had a degree or not. He didn't put a lot of stock in things like that. He loved me for who I was. He respected me. He would have been proud of me for going back to school — even if it was only a junior college."

Andrew swallowed hard, and his heart pounded in his chest until he felt like it would explode. "I'm so sorry. I . . ."

"Except for my kids, I'm alone. Up until now, I've been doing the best I could to get by, no thanks to you. I may not be the smartest woman in the world, but until today, I've given this my best shot. Apparently my best wasn't good enough for you."

Andrew's heart sank to his toes. How could he begin to redeem this? "I'm a tough teacher. Maybe a little too tough; I don't know. But I'm really sorry if I've said anything to hurt you. We can work this out."

"I don't want to work it out. I'm tired of trying. So I'm dropping your class, Mr. Dougherty. Isn't that what you wanted? You've won." Defeat covered her like a shroud.

I haven't won. Neither of us has won. I've caused this — caused her to fail. But how can I stop her? "Laura, please don't."

"That news should make you happy. I'm not going to be around to make fun of anymore."

He never had a chance to respond. She turned to walk in the opposite direction.

Laura made her way to the car, jaw clenched. She just wanted to leave and never come back. She couldn't blame it on the school. Her other classes were going well. Even the younger students all treated her with respect and dignity. It was only *him* — only that professor. *Why do I let him get to me? What is it about him that bothers me so much? He's not worth it. The class isn't worth it.*

Laura climbed in the car and rested her head on the steering wheel in defeat. "Now what?" she asked herself. She knew the consequences of dropping the class. It meant she couldn't possibly get the degree within the two-year period. It messed up everything. *He* messed up everything. Her thoughts deepened from melancholy to hopelessness. Without a degree, she would never make it out of her dead-end job. *Unless they fire me, of course.*

September 28. Looks like I might not make it through the day, after all. The tears began to flow. Frustrations were mounting. And now, thanks to Mr. Dougherty, the sky was falling.

CHAPTER 8

"Come on, Matt — just tell me," Andrew coaxed the young man in the admissions office. "I just need Laura Chapman's work number so I can call her about something that happened today after class."

"Why are you so hard on everyone?" Matt asked. "Why don't you just give this one a break?"

"Is that what everyone thinks — that I'm too hard on people?"

Matt smiled. "Well, yeah."

Andrew shook his head, miserable. "I really need to apologize, but I can't if you won't give me the information."

"You're gonna humble yourself and do the right thing, eh?" Matt said. "Think you'll regret it?"

"Probably not." He couldn't possibly regret anything more than he did the mess he'd gotten himself into already.

Matt typed a few words into the computer.

"Here you go," he said finally. "She works at the Bookstop on Tully. The number's right here."

"She works in a bookstore?" Interesting.

"Yeah. Do you want the number or not?"

"Sure. Sure." Andrew quickly scribbled down the number, but he'd already decided on a better plan. A bookstore. What a logical place for a college professor to turn up. Nothing contrived. He would simply be one in a number of shoppers, especially in a store the size of the Bookstop. Maybe, just maybe, he would find her there.

Laura drove up to the store, anxious to get inside and start working. The harder she worked, she reasoned, the quicker she could put this afternoon's incident out of her mind. And that's exactly what she had to do in order to maintain her sanity.

"Laura, everything all right?" Madeline asked.

"Yeah. Rough day." She opted not to elaborate. "But I'm fine. Really. I want you to know things are going to be better, Madeline. With me, I mean."

"What do you mean?"

"I mean," she said, with a look of determination, "I'm going to drop a class or two, and that should relieve my schedule a little."

Madeline will appreciate this news. She, of all people, knows how stressed I am.

"But your plans . . ."

"Never mind my plans," Laura asserted, putting on her best face. "I'm going to be fine; just wait and see. Now, what needs to be done?" There would be no time to dwell on the day's events if she had her mind on her work.

"Well, I've been thinking of revamping the inspirational section," her boss said. "That area's not getting a lot of business, and I think maybe it's because of the way we've got it set up."

Laura nodded. "Sounds great." Just the titles alone in the inspirational section would cheer her up. She moved forward, into a newer, brighter day. She would put Mr. Dougherty and this whole fiasco out of her mind.

Andrew pulled up to the Bookstop and anxiously looked toward the door. He glanced at his reflection in the rearview mirror before getting out, wet his fingers, and ran them through the lopsided curl in the center of his forehead that never seemed to lie down. *Useless.*

He made the short walk to the entrance of the large store. A poster in the window advertised Grisham's latest book. Looked like they were also having a sale on art books. None of that interested him at this moment. Only one thing captivated his mind: He had to find Laura Chapman.

Laura pulled books off the dusty top shelf with a little more force than usual, placing them onto the cart in front of her. She looked around her, trying to imagine what this section would look like in a few hours. With her help, it could be a showcase. This area could be improved in so many ways. What they needed were posters and promos, drawing people to this corner of the store. Perhaps a center table with inspirational best-sellers available at a glance.

Laura thumbed through a few of the books on the cart. Some of them looked a little dull, but others really caught her eye. One in particular stood out — *Put Your Troubles in the Blender and Give Them a Spin*. She didn't recognize the author's name, but she could certainly relate to the title. Who would have thought inspirational books could be humorous? She gave it a once-over. The text was clever, funny — yet packed a real punch in the emotional department. *Lord, are You trying to tell me something?*

■ ■ ■ ■

Andrew wound his way through the book-shelves, nervously looking for Laura. He rehearsed the words over and over again in his mind — what he would say when he saw her. He would start with a practical apology. He owed her that. He would then shift into an explanation of why he had said what he had. He would do his best not to further damage his case. Rather, he'd try to make himself look like the reasonable man that he was. Being a reasonable woman, she would respond in kind.

At least he hoped she would. He rounded a corner, practically running into a cart full of books. *Looks like I've found her. Now who's running into whom?* He smiled warmly, attempting to regain his composure.

Laura glanced his direction, her face falling. "What are you doing here?"

"Me?" He tried to look calm. "I come here a lot, actually. Interesting you should work here."

"Very."

"Laura —"

"Ms. Chapman." She stressed the words.

"C-H-A-P-M-A-N." His meager attempt at humor didn't seem to go over very well.

She didn't smile. "Look, Ms. Chapman, I really felt like we needed to talk. Do you have a few minutes?" His heart pounded in his ears, making it difficult to hear her response. He watched her lips as she spoke.

"I think we've covered all the basics, don't you?"

She has a point, but won't she even give me a chance? "I just wanted to say how sorry I am."

A baffled look crossed her face as he forged ahead. His gaze shifted to the ground. "I'm so sorry. I don't want you to quit the class. I really don't." He meant it. He hated to see any student give up, truth be told, but there was something special about this one. She needed to get through this — for psychological reasons as well as any other.

"I have to work and I really don't have time to deal with this. I'm going through enough at home and here at the store."

"What do you mean?" Nosiness kicked in. There seemed to be so much he didn't know about her, about Jessica.

"Never mind," she said, moving toward the door.

Just be direct. Get to the point. "So, will you come back?"

"Why should I?"

93

"I just hoped —" No, he wouldn't go that far. He didn't want to let her know that he had grown accustomed to seeing her, looked forward to every class with her.

"Can you give me one logical reason why I should come back to your class, Mr. Dougherty?" Laura asked, her face set.

Should he tell her that he enjoyed seeing her there, that she brought a smile to his face with her wit and her persistence? Should he let her know how impressed he was by the effort she took to raise her kids, work, and go to school? "I, uh . . ." He started, then hesitated slightly as fear caught hold of his tongue.

She shook her head in disbelief. "I thought so."

Laura watched as Dougherty sauntered out of the door, making his way to an old sedan with worn black paint. The car suited him — outdated and not terribly pretty. He deserved a car like that. She watched as he pulled out of the parking lot and sped down Tully with tires squealing.

Laura immediately set her mind back on her work. So much needed to be done, and she had lost time — thanks to him. He had quite a way of spoiling things. She quickly moved back toward the inspirational section, ready to dive in headfirst. She picked up a Bible to place it on the cart with the others. Her fingers lingered across the cover. It had been weeks since she picked up her own Bible to read. Somehow, just holding one now made her feel better.

She turned it open to the New Testament, her fingers racing along the words. They were as familiar as an old friend, and yet stirred an emotion in her she was unprepared for. Her index finger rested on a verse in 2 Corinthians that startled her. She couldn't remember ever reading it before.

"If anyone has caused grief, he has not so much grieved me as he has grieved all of you, to some extent — not to put it too severely. The punishment inflicted on him by the majority is sufficient for him. Now instead, you ought to forgive and comfort him, so that he will not be overwhelmed by excessive sorrow."

"'Forgive and comfort him?" She spoke the words softly, struck by their simplicity. But it couldn't be that easy! Laura closed the Bible quickly, placing it on the cart. Surely she wasn't supposed to comfort a man like Professor Dougherty. He was beyond help.

But, then again, why had he come here? Her mind began to drift to their conversation. Did he really feel bad about what he had said, or were there darker forces at work?

Madeline walked up.

"I guess you pretty much figured out who that was," Laura said.

"The infamous professor. Yeah, I've got it — and I hope you don't mind my saying this, but he doesn't seem like the ogre you made him out to be. He's a cutie."

Laura groaned — loudly, for effect.

Madeline grinned. "What did he want, anyway?"

"Actually, he wanted to apologize and asked me to come back to the class."

"Are you going to?" A smile made its way to her boss's lips. "I mean, I'm just saying if I had a professor who looked like that, I'd go back."

Laura thought carefully about her words before answering. "If I do, it won't have anything to do with him. I'd be going back for myself."

"Good girl. I'm proud of you."

"You are? I thought you didn't like the idea. Balancing work and school is a real pain."

"Like the idea? I'm so proud of you, I could burst! You make me want to go back myself."

"I do?"

"You do."

"Well," Laura said with a sigh, "it's a lot tougher than they make it out to be. I'm not sure how I'm ever going to get through this American History class if I do go back."

Madeline's eyes began to sparkle immediately. "Oh, Laura!" She grabbed her cell phone and lifted it triumphantly. "I have the most amazing idea!"

CHAPTER 9

Laura sat in the college cafeteria, clutching her colorful American History book. She slowly worked her way through a chapter on indentured servants, fascinated by the material. She glanced up occasionally, slightly distracted. She looked back and forth — from her book, to her watch, to all of the people. The noisy room provided some degree of comfort — trays clattering, soda cans popping open, students chattering incessantly — these were all things she had grown to love. Even so, Laura found it very difficult to focus. The whole thing was nerve-wracking, especially under the circumstances.

"Come on, come on."

He should be here soon. She took a bite of her sandwich and chased it down with a mouthful of soda, then glanced at her watch nervously. *Not much time left. He'd better come quickly, or there really won't be much point to all of this.* She tried to keep her attention on the chapter but found it extremely difficult. She stared at her watch as the minutes ticked by. *He should definitely be here.*

"Are you Laura Chapman?" A deep voice rang out.

Laura looked up into the twinkling eyes of a gentleman with peppered hair and a well-trimmed gray beard. "I am," she answered. "And you must be Richard."

"Dick DeHart," he responded, extending his hand for a firm handshake. "Madeline says you need some help in history."

"Help is an understatement," she confessed. *How much should I confide in him?* Then again, it might be better to let him know what he was up against. She spoke hesitantly. "If I don't pass this course, I might as well drop out of school."

"Well, we can't have that, can we?" He sat next to her then pulled his chair a bit closer. "You've come to the right place."

She couldn't help but notice his dimples, not hidden in the slightest by his beard. He was a nice-looking man, just as Madeline had said — probably fifty-two or fifty-three, somewhere in that neighborhood. Not that it mattered. It was just that Laura had looked for a tutor in her own age group, not from among the students at Wainesworth. Things were rough enough this way.

"I don't know what my sister told you about me," Richard explained, "but I used to teach here at the college until about three years ago. That's when my wife passed away."

"I'm so sorry," Laura said. "I'm a widow, myself. In fact, my husband has been gone three years, too."

"Really?" He looked more than a little interested.

Laura immediately grew nervous.

"I think I've seen you at the store a couple of times. I've been doing a lot of research."

"What sort of research?"

"History, naturally," he said excitedly. "I've taken to writing college textbooks since I left the teaching profession."

"That's fascinating." Madeline had simply described him as a history buff.

"In fact," Richard said, pointing to her American History text, "I had a hand in writing that book."

"You wrote this textbook?" she asked, turning to the cover for a quick glance. Sure enough, *Richard DeHart & Jonathan Frisk* jumped off of the cover at her. "For heaven's sake."

"I had a particularly tough time with that

chapter you were reading when I walked up." He reached for the book. "May I?"

"Of course!"

"You're just starting the unit on slavery, right?"

"That's right." She looked at the open book with new admiration and respect. "Why did you have a tough time?"

"There's a shortage of documents concerning slave groups brought over from the Caribbean." He frowned. "I wanted to include a well-researched section on their story, but I couldn't track down everything I needed. What you're reading there is just a shell of what I had hoped to include."

"Looks pretty thorough to me," Laura observed.

"Still, we may have to do a second edition. There's just so much material to cover."

"If you don't mind my saying so, there's plenty of material in this book as it is. Getting through it in one semester is going to be rough. And Dougherty — well, he's not making my life any easier."

"Professor Andrew Dougherty?"

Laura nodded.

Richard let out a whistle and shook his head.

"You know him?"

"Know him? We used to be archenemies — seemed to be an ongoing battle over who could be the better teacher. Also, there was that *dean* issue."

"Dean issue?" She grew more curious by the moment.

"Well, yeah," he said, "but I hate to talk about it. I was named dean of the History Department here at Wainesworth about five years back. Apparently Dougherty felt I had one-upped him. I don't know that he ever quite forgave me."

"Sounds like he carries a lot of grudges," Laura said. "Actually, that's part of my problem. . . ."

"Got on his bad side right away, did you?" Richard laughed.

She nodded, embarrassed. "Yeah, but it really wasn't my fault."

"It rarely is. Dougherty's got a real chip on his shoulder. But you're barely two months into the school year. There's plenty of time left in the semester to make things even worse."

"Very funny. But I'm serious. He hates me."

"Hate is a pretty strong word," Richard said, suddenly looking serious. "Besides, I think he's just covering for something."

"Covering for something?" He must know

quite a few things about Andrew Dougherty that she didn't. Not that she cared.

"I think he must have had his heart broken somewhere along the way," Richard said with a sly grin. "At least that's what I've gathered."

Really. Interesting tidbit of information. For the life of her, Laura couldn't imagine any woman entering a relationship with a man like that.

"Well, let's forget about our dear Professor Dougherty, shall we?" Dick pulled his chair even closer. "Looks like we've got our work cut out for us."

"Yes, we do." She tried to sound confident, but the smell of his cologne distracted her. Greg had worn the same brand in their earlier years together. Somehow, just the aroma made her feel a little out of sorts.

"I think we should go over this unit before you head into class today." He pointed to the book.

"You're right." She turned her attention to the chapter on slavery. It looked, for once, like she had a logical, workable plan.

Andrew entered the cafeteria, hoping for a quick bite to eat before teaching his last class of the day. *What a madhouse.* The sights, sounds, and smells were dizzying, making him claustrophobic and completely uncomfortable. He needed order, control. What had made him think grabbing a baked potato and soda would be easy? Nothing proved to be easy here.

He forced his way through the mob, heading to the counter. "Oh, excuse me," he said, as he bumped into the back of a chair. He looked down instinctively. Only then did he realize Laura Chapman's eyes gazed directly into his. "Laura . . ."

She didn't respond immediately. Instead, her gaze shifted to the man sitting next to her.

Richard DeHart. What's he doing here? Andrew hesitantly extended his hand. "De-Hart."

"Professor Dougherty." Dick shook it with a firm grip.

"What are you doing here?" It was a fair question. After all, the man didn't teach at the school anymore.

"Ms. Chapman has asked me to tutor her."

"In history?" Talk about throwing a kink into his plans to offer to help Laura. This guy had no business . . .

"Naturally," Richard said. "What did you think?"

Andrew looked back and forth between

Laura and Richard. Something about the combination almost made him feel sick. He sought out Laura's eyes. "How did you two meet? If you don't mind my asking."

She looked up at him with a confident smile. "Richard's sister is my boss, Madeline."

"That's right," Dick said. "She told me about Laura's plight, and I rushed right over."

Laura's plight? What is that supposed to mean? Andrew's heart quickened a beat, looking at the two of them together. Not that Dick DeHart was a bad guy. He was great. Maybe a little too great.

Laura observed the look of confusion on Professor Dougherty's face. "Richard tells me he wrote our text." She closed the book and held it up under Andrew's watchful eye.

"Yeah. Knew that."

Great show of support for his colleague. "We were just discussing this week's chapter. I'm finding it very enlightening." *That might be stretching it just a bit.*

"Are you?" He didn't sound very convinced.

"We were just about to enter a lively discussion on indentured servants," Richard

105

added. "Would you like to join us, Dougherty?"

"No, thank you." He looked at Laura but spoke more to Richard. "I, uh — I've got a ton of other things to take care of. And then I have to teach a class. I still do that, you know."

They stared at each other until Laura grew uncomfortable. She turned her glance to the textbook in question, trying to change the direction of the conversation. "This is so well written," she commented, pointing to a particular passage. "How did you ever think to phrase it that way?"

Richard's eyes beamed. He spoke in earnest. "I just felt passionate about the subject matter and wanted to express it in the most ardent way I could so that the reader would be drawn into the discussion. That's all."

"Good grief." Andrew turned on his heels to leave.

"Sure you won't join us, Dougherty?" Richard called out, a smile crossing his lips.

"No, thank you." He turned to walk in the direction of the counter, leaving her to face Richard DeHart alone.

"That's the one," Regina said, looking Andrew in the eye.

"I beg your pardon?" He followed her finger until his gaze fell on Laura Chapman.

"That's the one I've got picked out for you."

"Oh no, not that one. Anyone else but her!"

"Why not?" Regina asked, insulted. "Not good enough for you?"

"It's not that. She's just — well, she and I don't exactly get along."

"I'm sure it's your fault. She seems like a nice enough lady."

"Thanks a lot."

She smiled. "Even though your heart is in the right place, your people skills are a little lacking."

"Meaning I'm not really the tyrant everyone thinks I am?"

"Of course not. But you've changed the subject. I want to talk about finding you a wife. Thank goodness you have me; otherwise I don't know what you'd do."

"I don't need a wife," he said defiantly.

"You don't need all that butter and sour cream, either," Regina said, pointing to his baked potato, "but I notice you're still eating it."

Laura looked up from her conversation with Dick DeHart, her gaze resting on Andrew

Dougherty. He remained deep in conversation with a woman across the counter. She had dark hair and complexion and looked to be in her early forties. *A real beauty.* Not that it made a difference.

Laura noticed they had been talking for quite awhile. An odd mixture of emotions shot through her. More than anything, she found herself extremely intrigued by the woman. How could any female on the planet look that comfortable with Andrew Dougherty?

CHAPTER 10

Andrew passed out the exams, pausing as he placed one on Laura Chapman's desk. Nearly three weeks had passed since that awful day when she threatened to quit his class. Each day he breathed another sigh of relief when she walked in the door. However, he had mixed emotions when it came to her sudden and obvious association with Richard DeHart. *I can't stand that guy. What a lady's man.* Laura Chapman certainly didn't need that in her life. *Wait a minute. I've got no right analyzing what Laura Chapman does and doesn't need. It's none of my business.*

Still . . .

He glanced down at her wavy hair, his hand accidentally brushing against it as he handed a paper to the girl on her left.

"Sorry," he said quietly. Truthfully, he wasn't sorry. One touch had been enough to send sparks through him. Just the thought of it scared him to death.

Laura reached up instinctively, her fingers pushing through the spot where the professor's hand brushed against her hair. It had been an accident, surely, but his lingering gaze left her more than a little curious. Irritated, she turned away from him. She was about to prove a point — a very strong point.

"You may begin." Professor Dougherty gave the go-ahead.

Lord, help me. She turned the paper over and began to read through the questions — first, with fear; then with overwhelming relief. She knew this stuff. A couple of questions might present a challenge, but they were essay questions. Surely she could come up with something for those. As for the multiple-choice questions, they would be a piece of cake.

Laura looked up at Andrew's desk, where he sat silently grading papers. He seemed lost in his work. She turned back to the questions, breathing a huge sigh of relief. At one point, she glanced across the room to where Jessica sat, stone-faced, staring at her exam paper. Try as she might, Laura had not been able to get her daughter to study with her.

She focused on the test, answering questions rapidly and accurately. A short time later, she walked to Professor Dougherty's desk and dropped the exam into the appropriate basket with a smile. She had a lot to smile about. For once, she'd actually accomplished her goal. She'd proven, at least to herself, that she could excel. Soon enough, he would know it, too.

The professor looked confused. For a moment Laura felt a twinge of guilt, though she couldn't quite figure out why. She had nothing to feel guilty about. *I've done all of the right things, so why do I feel so bad?*

Dick DeHart had turned out to be a regular Romeo. Picking up on the fact that he seemed interested in far more than her mind, she carefully chose when and where they would meet to study. *I could never be interested in a man like him.*

Her gaze fell on Andrew Dougherty once again. His rumpled hair stuck up on his head. He wore a mismatched shirt and tie, and his pants had gone out of style years ago.

Still . . . he did have a certain charm about him. He looked up at her with a smile and she almost returned it. Almost.

Andrew waited until the classroom cleared

before shuffling through the stack of exams to find the one he was looking for. "Miller, Johnson, Tanner, Breckenridge . . . Chapman." Ah yes. Laura Chapman's exam. He scanned it quickly and made it to the bottom of the first page. No errors so far. He turned to page two. Flawless. A little glitch in an essay question on page three — worth about two or three points at most, but page four appeared to be perfect. She'd aced the exam. Aced it.

Amazed, he checked it once again. Only one conclusion could be drawn: Her study sessions with DeHart had been effective. Very effective. That confirmed something he'd worried about for days. She and Dick DeHart must have spent a lot of time together.

A twinge of jealousy shot through him, stirring up an odd mixture of emotions. *I'm so proud of her. She's turned out to be a much harder worker than I gave her credit for.* But on the other hand, how could she give so much of her time and attention to someone as unscrupulous as DeHart? He struggled with the thought. *Maybe she hasn't figured him out yet. Maybe someone needs to warn her.* Andrew tossed ideas about, clearly confused over the whole thing. If her academic performance improved with Dick's help, how could he possibly go about approaching her now?

Laura heard the ringing of the phone as she turned the key in the front door. "Come on, come on . . ." She struggled to get the door open. By the fourth ring, she made it into the living room. "Hello?" She dropped the armload of books, still panting.

"Ms. Chapman?"

A man's voice — probably one of those annoying telemarketers. They called a lot. She glanced at the Caller ID. "Unavailable."

Oh, why did I even pick it up? "Yes?"

"I was hoping to catch you." Why did the man's voice sound so familiar? "I've been meaning to talk to you about your work in my class."

Bingo. Andrew Dougherty. What in the world did he want with her? Her hands began to tremble. She forced her voice to remain calm as she clutched the receiver. "What about my work?"

"I'm really pleased with it. In fact, I just graded your exam."

"So soon?" Something must have happened to prompt this.

"Uh, yes. You got a ninety-seven."

Ninety-seven? That's awesome! And yet, she wouldn't let her jubilation show. She couldn't. "Well, thank you for letting me know." She tried to keep her voice on an even keel. "Though I'm not sure why you took the time to call. You could have just told me in class."

"I'm pleased with your grade," he continued, "but . . ."

"But what?"

"Well, to be honest, I was hoping to talk with you about Dick DeHart."

"Oh?"

"I just think you need to know that De-Hart has a . . . well, a past." He seemed to be choosing his words very carefully.

"A past? What does that have to do with anything?" Laura grew angrier by the moment. "This is really none of your business."

"I just thought you might like to know."

"I'm not interested in gossip, Professor. In fact, I'm stunned that you are. To be perfectly frank, if I had anything to say about Mr. DeHart to you, it would all be good." Granted, Dick DeHart acted a little too close over the last couple of weeks, but she certainly wasn't ready to admit that to Andrew Dougherty. "He's gracious and kind," she continued, "and seems to see something of value in me. It's clear he has my best wishes at heart."

"Among other things."

"I beg your pardon?"

"His reputation precedes him, Laura."

"Ms. Chapman."

"Ms. Chapman," he said slowly, deliberately, "I've got your best interest at heart. Really, I do."

"Well, thank you just the same, but —"

"If I were you —"

"Well, you're not," she said emphatically. She had just about reached wit's end with this guy dabbling in her personal life. She wouldn't allow it. "Besides, this is really none of your business, Professor."

"Fine."

"Fine," she echoed. "Was that all you were calling about?"

"That's all."

"Well, if it's all the same to you, I really need to hang up. I've still got to work today. Good-bye, Mr. Dougherty."

"Ms. Chapman."

With a click, he disappeared. Laura still clutched the phone in her sweaty hand. She slammed it back down, shifting her gaze to the books she'd carelessly tossed on the coffee table. The American History book sat at the top of the stack, a grim reminder that this battle had just begun.

Irritated, she shoved the book to the bottom of the stack.

■ ■ ■ ■

Andrew stared at the receiver, dumb-
founded. *There's no winning with this woman.*
Yet he couldn't get those amazing eyes
and wavy brown hair out of his mind.

CHAPTER 11

"You want to what?" Laura turned to face Dick DeHart, who had come into the store for a visit.

"I want to take you out to a movie this Saturday night." He slipped his arm across her shoulder.

"But I . . ." Uncomfortable, she pulled away from his embrace. Laura couldn't seem to get the professor's words out of her mind — something about Richard DeHart's past. She had no idea what he meant, but she wasn't taking any chances.

"There's a great new movie out on the Civil War," Dick said, giving her what looked to be a rehearsed pout. "We could look at it as an educational date."

"I'm not sure I'm up to any kind of a 'date,' " Laura said. "I'm just not ready for that yet."

"Well, we don't have to call it a date, then," he argued. "We could go to dinner afterwards and have a, uh — a study session."

Laura had seen just about enough of his study sessions already. She spoke very candidly. "I don't think so, but thanks for the offer."

"Aw, come on, Laurie," he wooed.

"It's Laura."

"You know you want to spend time with me. I'm irresistible."

"Is that what you think?" she asked incredulously. "You think I'm that easily swayed?" *He's got to be kidding.*

"You're a woman." He shrugged. "That about says it all, doesn't it?"

Laura's blood began to boil. She couldn't stand men with an attitude like this. She hadn't tolerated it in the professor, and she wouldn't in this man either.

"I may be a woman" — Laura tried to keep her voice steady — "but that doesn't mean I don't know how to use sound judgment and reason. I'm perfectly capable of doing that."

His expression never changed. "Aw, come on," he coaxed. "I didn't mean anything by that comment. Let's go out Saturday night and have a good time. We'll paint the town red. I promise to have you back home before you lose your glass slipper."

"I don't think so." Laura turned back to her work. "In fact, I don't think I'll be needing any more tutoring sessions either. I'm doing pretty well on my own."

"Sure you are. Just like you were before I came along."

Laura stared at him in disbelief. *This guy is too much.*

"You'll change your mind." He turned to leave. "And when you do — call me."

She wouldn't call him. She would never call him.

Andrew signed onto the Internet and scrolled through his e-mail — junk mail, a letter from a colleague, and a quick note from his friend, Joe, asking if he'd be interested in going to a high school football game Saturday night to watch his son play.

A high school football game? Andrew barely tolerated sports, and the idea of sitting out in the cold to watch a bunch of kids toss a ball around sounded anything but inviting. Still, Joe was his friend, and he owed him for the blind date thing. Might as well balance the scales by going. "Why not?" Andrew said aloud. He had little else to do, anyway.

"Mom, the homecoming game is Saturday

night." Kent sounded nervous.

"Do you have a date?" She gazed into her son's eyes as she posed the question. He looked too young to even consider dating, and yet the inevitable seemed to be upon her.

"Yeah, I'm going with Mandy. The dance is after the game. That's what I wanted to talk to you about."

"She needs a mum, right?" It wouldn't be the first red-and-white mum she'd made over the years.

"Yeah." He looked like a nervous wreck. "I need it by Friday morning."

Laura smiled, realizing this would be Kent's first school dance. Her heart began to ache, realizing that Greg wouldn't be here, snapping pictures as he had so often in the past as Jessica headed out the door.

"You'll have it by Friday morning," she promised.

"Great. But that's not all."

"What else?"

"The band is playing at the game. Are you coming?"

A football game? *Lord, you know I can't stand football. Surely You wouldn't ask me to do that.* "I don't know, Kent . . ."

"Aw, come on, Mom," he argued. "You go to all of Jessica's piano recitals."

120

He had a point there.

"I guess so, but I might leave after half-time. I have a lot of homework this weekend."

"That's cool." Kent smiled. "Just as long as you watch me play the trumpet, you can go whenever you want."

He bounded from the room with his usual zest, and she was left alone with her books and her thoughts. Not that she minded. It had been a long day, and the silence felt just right.

Andrew slipped into bed for the night, television still running. A sappy love story played itself out on the screen. Whether he meant for it to happen or not, he found his attention glued to the set.

"Aw, don't do it, man," he said to the character on the screen. "Don't give your heart away to her. She's not worth it."

He stared in disbelief as the man in the movie told the young woman that he loved her. She responded by slapping him in the face.

"I tried to tell you." Andrew shook his head. "But you wouldn't listen."

What's wrong with women these days? That's all Andrew really wanted to know. What did they want? And how in the world could any man ever succeed in being everything they expected him to be? He quickly snapped off the TV, determined to put females out of his mind. Unfortunately, when he closed his eyes, all he could see was Laura Chapman's face. She had an amazing smile — when she bothered to smile — and the cutest dimples he'd seen in ages. How could he possibly go about winning a woman like her? He didn't stand a chance in the world.

Andrew wrestled with the sheets, trying to get comfortable. Would there ever be someone — anyone — to call his own? Perhaps some people just weren't meant to have love in their lives. Maybe that was part of some sort of master plan. Who knew?

His mind reeled back to Karen instinctively. She had been so ideal, so perfect. And yet she hurt him. Terribly.

"We all make mistakes," he whispered to himself as he remembered some of the words he'd spoken to Laura in those first few days of school. He had been deliberately cruel. Even Karen, in breaking his heart, hadn't acted maliciously. She'd simply followed her heart.

Suddenly, lying in the stillness of his room, Andrew Dougherty managed to forgive the woman who had broken his heart fifteen years ago. For the first time, he felt completely free to love again.

CHAPTER 12

Laura put the finishing touches on the red-and-white mum, then handed it to Kent.

"Looks great, Mom." He held it gingerly, as if afraid it might break.

"It ought to," she responded. "I had to mortgage the house to buy all that stuff." *A slight exaggeration — but only slight.* "What time is the game tomorrow night? I'm hoping Jess and Nathan will want to come with me."

"Seven-thirty." He bit into a muffin then spoke with full mouth. "You gonna leave after halftime?"

"It depends on how the team is playing," she said with a chuckle. "Nah. If I leave, it will only be because I've got a lot of —"

"I know," he interrupted. "You've got a lot of homework. Trust me, I understand."

"Just promise me this." Laura looked at her son with as firm an expression as she could manage. "Promise me you'll do your best not to get into any trouble."

"It's cool, Mom. I'm fine."

"I sure hope so." She gave him a peck on the cheek. "Get on out of here. Go to school." He headed out the door, whistling as he went.

Thank You, Lord. He's doing so much better! As he left with the mum in hand, she couldn't help but think of the one she'd worn her senior year in high school, so many years ago. It had been blue and white, a gift from Greg. His mother had worked diligently on it. To this day, it hung in her closet, though the cloth flower had faded over the years.

"Mom?" Jessica's voice sounded surprisingly sweet.

She turned to face her. "Good morning, Jess."

"Mom, I was wondering if you'd like to go to breakfast with me."

"Breakfast?"

"Yeah," Jess said with a smile. "I need to talk to you and thought I might do it over breakfast. Sound good?"

Laura smiled, in spite of herself. Jessica wanted to spend time with her. A first — in quite awhile, anyway. How could she turn that down?

"I'd be delighted. Where do you want to go?"

"Your choice, but this is my treat. I've still got a little birthday money left from Grandma."

"Okay then," Laura said, standing. "Pancake House on the freeway. Their waffles are incredible. Blueberry pancakes —"

"With blueberry syrup," Jess added with a smile. "I know. I remember."

"Why the celebration?"

"You'll see, you'll see. Go get dressed and let me get you out of here for a little while." Jessica looked anxious. Something must be up. Suddenly Laura knew the answer. It had something to do with the piano scholarship. Jessica had gotten the news she'd been waiting on and wanted to share it with her.

"Are you sure?" Laura could hardly contain her excitement.

"Yep. I'm sure."

Laura bounded off to her bedroom, erupting five minutes later in a sweater and slacks.

"Better?"

"Much better," her daughter said, smiling.

Fifteen minutes later, they sat in a corner booth of the Pancake House, sipping cups of hot coffee. *What a wonderful treat!* Laura hadn't felt this spoiled in ages.

126

"Mom, I need to tell you something." Jessica looked serious for a change.

Laura's heart began to pound instantly. *Why do I always assume the worst?*

"Don't look so scared."

"What is it?" *Whatever it is, I can take it.*

"Well, you know that I planned to audition for the piano scholarship, right?"

"Planned to?"

"Well, I . . ."

"What, honey?" Laura asked. "You can say it."

"I couldn't do it, Mom. I was too scared to go in and play."

"You what?" Laura felt stunned. "But you've waited for that audition for weeks. You didn't even go in?"

Her daughter's beautiful face fell immediately. Laura knew she should try to be more understanding, but once the words started, she just couldn't seem to help herself.

"She can't stand me," Andrew said as he sat across from Regina in the nearly empty lunchroom. With no classes scheduled today, only faculty and staff drifted in and out. Regina took advantage of the break, plopping down onto the chair across from him at the lunch table.

"Oh, pooh!" Regina said. "She just doesn't know you yet."

"No, she knows me. And she really can't stand me." Andrew sighed deeply. "I tried to call her."

"You called her?" Regina asked excitedly. "To ask her out?"

"No, of course not. I just wanted to talk to her about her grades."

"Oh." Regina's face fell. "Well, that was a romantic touch."

"You don't understand." He felt his shoulders sag in defeat. "It's not that easy for me. I don't know how to talk to a woman."

"You're talking to me."

"That's different." Surely she could see that.

She gave him a look. "What's that supposed to mean?"

"I mean, you're like a sister to me — not like a woman."

"Well, thanks a lot."

"I can't say anything right."

"I sure hope you do a better job than that when you're talking to her, or the game will be over before it even starts."

"It's already over," he said, standing. "And we're not even in the second quarter yet."

Laura struggled through the afternoon at

work, her thoughts in a jumbled mess. *Jessica didn't get the scholarship.* The words went round and round in her head, disappointment filling her.

"I, uh . . ." Laura shook her head, not wanting to talk. The knot in her throat wouldn't allow it anyway.

"That's all right," Madeline said. "I'm just worried about you, that's all. This doesn't have anything to do with my brother, does it?"

Laura laughed, in spite of herself. "No," she said, grateful for the relief the laughter brought. "Nothing to do with your brother."

"That's good," her boss said. "Because I thought for a minute there, I was going to have to hurt him. You just let me know."

Let her know? Should she let her know her brother had one thing, and only one thing, on his mind — and it wasn't American history?

"Would you mind taking over the register?" Madeline asked. "I need to check a new shipment that just came in."

"No problem." Laura headed to the cash register, her mind still reeling.

Jessica didn't get the scholarship. The words still tossed themselves around in her head. She shouldn't be this disappointed, but money didn't grow on trees, and with two of them in college, things might get tight by the spring.

"Uh, umm . . ." A man in front of her cleared his throat, trying to get her attention. "Are you going to wait on me or not?"

"Oh, I'm sorry. My mind is on other things."

"That's obvious."

"Will this be all?" She glanced down at the book he'd placed on the counter: *One Hundred Ways to Become a Better Person.* Intriguing title. She would have to remember to look at it later.

"Yeah, that's all." He pushed the book toward her. "My wife says I have to read this."

"Really." She didn't mean it in an accusing way, but he glared at her, just the same. "Well, I hope you enjoy it. That will be $22.95 plus tax — a total of $24.78."

"That's a lot of money just to become a better person," he grumbled, reaching for a credit card.

"I'm sure you're worth it, sir."

He smiled warmly — for the first time. "Yeah, I guess I am. Who knows? Maybe this book will help."

"If it does," she said, "come back in and let me know so I can buy a copy for myself."

The gentleman headed toward the door,

his expression totally changed from when they had begun.

"Looks like you had a nice effect on him," Madeline said, returning with a tracking slip in hand. "He's one of my worst customers. Comes in here every few months to buy another self-help book his wife has recommended."

"I've never seen him before. But he wasn't so bad, really. Sometimes people just . . ." She glanced at the floor. "Have a rough day." She smiled lamely at her boss, hoping for a positive response.

"Laura," Madeline said, looking at her intently, "it seems like nearly every day has been a rough one for you lately, but you're going to get through all of this. I know you are. You're a lot stronger than you think."

"Then why don't I feel it?"

"It doesn't matter what you feel. You just have to begin to act on it." Laura smiled warmly at her boss, thankful for the encouragement. *I sure hope you're right.*

CHAPTER 13

Kent bit into an apple, then spoke with his mouth full. "You didn't forget about the game tonight, did you, Mom?"

"No." She glanced through the refrigerator for something that might resemble lunch. There wasn't much to choose from — a stale package of bologna and a half-eaten can of sliced peaches. Neither sounded appetizing.

"You're gonna freeze to death if you stand there all day." He reached around her to grab a half-gallon of milk.

"Yeah, I know." She closed the door, opting to skip the food idea. *It's not like things aren't already cold enough in this house already.* Ever since her breakfast with Jessica yesterday morning, little more than a word or two had been spoken between them. *I need to apologize.* But every outward sign convinced her Jessica wasn't ready to hear it yet.

Kent poured a tall glass of milk then left the carton standing open on the counter. "Is Jess coming with you?"

"I don't think so."

"Bummer." It was only one word, but it genuinely reflected her feelings.

Andrew pulled his jacket out of the closet and slipped it on. For late October, today proved to be particularly chilly. *I don't know why I'm going, anyway. I've got no interest in football. What an illogical game.* Then again, Joe had been a good sport about the whole "Judy" thing, and his eldest, Jonathan, was like a son to Andrew. For that reason alone, Andrew would go. He would endure the crowd and the noise. He would put up with their lousy band and their childish bantering back and forth.

Andrew made the drive to the stadium with the radio playing softly in the background. A love song streamed from the radio. For some reason, a picture of Laura Chapman came to mind immediately — the way her hair framed her face, the richness of her smile every time she received a good grade. She seemed to be receiving a lot of those lately. Just thinking about her made him smile.

Laura made her way through the crowd, shivering. Already, she regretted her decision to wear a lightweight sweater instead of her heavy coat. She gazed out onto the field where cheerleaders warmed up. They leaped about like gazelles and shouted their chants, clearly ready for the game to begin.

It feels so awkward, coming here by myself. Almost as bad as sitting in a pew alone. She hadn't managed to do that for quite some time either. Her mind began to wander back to another game, just two years ago, when Jessica had been nominated for homecoming queen. *Greg would have been so proud.* Though their daughter hadn't won the coveted crown, she had certainly excelled above the other girls in Laura's eyes. *In every conceivable way, she was a queen that night.*

Just the thought of her daughter caused Laura's brow to wrinkle. The strain between them grew more with each day. The gap seemed wider than the football field below, and there didn't appear to be a way to narrow it.

"Andrew, over here!" Behind her, a man's voice rang out, almost deafening her. Laura looked up to find Professor Andrew Dougherty waving from a distance. Their eyes met. She immediate dropped her gaze to the ground. *Great.*

Andrew's heart skipped a beat the minute he saw Laura. She looked beautiful in her soft peach sweater. With her hair pulled back like that, she almost looked like a teenager. In fact, she looked remarkably like Jessica tonight. Should he tell her so? Would that be inappropriate? He made his way up the steps to her row, pausing momentarily to nod in her direction. She nodded back with less enthusiasm.

Joe acted a little more interested. "Glad you could make it," he said as he reached out to shake Andrew's hand. "I was starting to think you'd changed your mind."

Thank goodness I didn't. "Oh," he said finally, "I, uh . . . I got caught up in traffic." He sat quickly, gaze fixed on the back of Laura's head.

Truth was, he had pulled his car off the road to listen to the love song on the radio. It sparked something in him that he hadn't felt for some time. And now, the very one he'd been thinking about sat directly in front of him, completely alone. *This has to be more than coincidence. I'm not that lucky.*

Joe slapped him on the back. "You look like you're a million miles away tonight. Rough day?"

"No, not at all."

"Well, I hope you're ready for a great game. I hear they're playing a tough team tonight."

"Really? That's nice."

Joe laughed, slapping him on the back once again. "You're a laugh a minute. No wonder Judy never asks about you anymore." He erupted into laughter, and Andrew did everything in his power to change the subject, hopeful Laura hadn't heard.

"Who did you say they were playing again?" he asked as he looked toward the field.

"Westfield High. They're a tough team."

"Oh yeah. I've heard that." Not that he cared. Football was a sport he deliberately avoided.

"We'll whip 'em." The proud papa beamed.

"Speaking of 'we,' where's Jolene?" Andrew asked, looking around. He still chuckled, thinking of their names. Joe and Jolene. The all-American couple.

"Oh, she's at the junior high tonight," Joe answered with a shrug. "Brenna's in a play of some sort. You know how it is when

136

you've got a houseful of kids. You have to divide your time."

No, I don't know. Andrew often wondered if he ever would. He turned his attention back to Laura's hair. A soft breeze played with her tiny ponytail, causing the peach ribbon to dance around in the wind. He stared at it, fixated.

The field below came alive as the game got under way, yet Andrew just couldn't seem to concentrate on it. Laura's perfume pulled at him in a way that boggled his mind. *What is that smell — some sort of flower or something else?* He couldn't quite put his finger on it, but talk about alluring. *And that hair of hers — that amazing, wavy brown hair — it's making me a crazy man.* He wanted to run his fingers through it, to nuzzle close and smell it. *What's come over me? Is Laura Chapman some sort of unattainable dream? Do I really need a woman in my life?*

"Snap out of it!" he whispered to himself, shaking his head. *What am I doing, thinking about her that way? She's certainly not making any moves to communicate with me.*

Perhaps she had plans to meet someone. A fear gripped him as he considered the idea. Maybe Dick DeHart would take the place on the bench in front of him. Maybe he was already here. Maybe . . .

"Andrew, are you listening to me?" Joe's voice shocked him back to reality.

"I, uh . . ."

"Are you okay, man?" His friend looked concerned. "You're not acting like yourself."

"Yeah, yeah . . ."

"You're sure acting strange," Joe said. "I know what you need. You need food. I'm gonna go get a hot dog and a soft drink. You want the same?"

"Oh, sure," Andrew said as he fished for his wallet. "Whatever you say."

"What I say is, you're in need of some serious help, my friend." Joe flashed him a grin as he left. Andrew sat in silence, trying to decide what to do next. *Should I talk to her?*

Laura watched in silence as the professor's friend left the stands, realizing he sat alone behind her.

Please don't let him talk to me. The words flashed through her mind like an alarm going off. She couldn't bear another confrontation tonight. She'd been through enough over the last few days.

His voice interrupted her thoughts. "Laura, how are you?" *The moment of truth.*

"Fine." She glanced at him briefly. She

deliberately looked back down at the field, hoping he would take the hint. He didn't.

"I didn't realize you still had children in high school," he commented. Then he moved to sit next to her. *That took some nerve. What does he think he's doing?* Laura knew she should say something to him — make him go back to where he came from. She turned, prepared to do battle — but no words came out. Something about the way he wore his hair tonight seemed a little different, but she couldn't quite put her finger on it.

"Uh, yes," she said finally. "Well, just one. My son Kent is in the band." She pointed to the section below where red and white reigned alongside silver and gold instruments. Suddenly the cold air gripped her. She began to shake, and goose bumps made their way up each arm.

"You're cold!" Andrew pulled off his jacket. "Please, put this on."

"Oh no, I couldn't," she argued. He draped the coat over her shoulders and she instinctively pulled it tight, grateful for its warmth.

"Kent, did you say?" the professor asked with interest. "Which one is he?"

"He plays the trumpet. He's the one with

the brown hair on the end of the fourth row."

"Ah. He looks like you," the professor said with a nod. "Same hair."

She shrugged, still shivering. "I guess so."

"No, it is," he said firmly. "Your hair is brunette, just like his."

Brunette? It was brown — plain dull, boring brown. She'd never thought of it as anything else. Somehow "brunette" made it sound more intriguing.

"His hair looks a lot more like yours than Jessica's does," Andrew observed. "Her auburn hair isn't anything like yours."

Had he actually spent time thinking about this? The notion blew her away. "She takes after her father. Greg was a redhead." She inwardly scolded herself for talking about her husband to a man she barely knew.

"Ah, that would explain the temper, too," he said with a laugh.

"You think Jessica has a temper?" Her own quickly rose to the surface.

"And you don't?"

He has a point. Jess had even used that temper in his class a time or two to gain attention from him.

"I'll bet you're really proud of her."

"Sure. I'm proud of both of them." He had struck a nerve — flattering her kids.

Was he serious or just trying to smooth things over with her?

"No, I mean the news . . ."

"What news?"

"I just found out yesterday afternoon myself," he continued. "Of course, it's all over campus."

"What are you talking about?"

"The scholarship," he said, looking at her incredulously. "The music scholarship."

Laura's heart began to race. Something must be wrong here — very wrong. Just yesterday morning, Jessica sat across from her at breakfast, telling her that she *didn't* get the scholarship.

"That's not right," she said, shaking her head. "Jess didn't get the music scholarship. She didn't even audition. I know all about it."

He looked at her in disbelief. "Sure, she did. Her vocal coach, Barbara Nelson, is a friend of mine. We talk about Jess all the time. She's doing really well in her voice lessons."

"*Voice* lessons?" Laura struggled to maintain her composure. There must be some mistake here.

"Sure. They say she's a natural. Haskins was anxious to hear her the other day. From what I heard, she really knocked his socks

141

off. He said there was something about hearing that hymn sung with such depth that almost brought tears to his eyes."

Haskins? Hymn? Laura's head began to spin. She started to tremble uncontrollably but not from the cold. Her emotions were in a whirlwind. This made no sense at all. *Jessica is a pianist. She went to audition for a piano scholarship. When did she start taking voice lessons?* To be honest, Laura had been so busy, she wasn't sure what classes her daughter had signed up for.

"Haskins?" she stammered.

"Sure. The choral director. He was very impressed — said she sounded like she'd been singing for years."

"Singing for years . . ." Laura's voice trailed off. *This is awful.*

"That Haskins really knows his stuff, so she must be good. He told Barbara that he might be willing to commend Jess for the Houston Grand Opera's Youth program if she continues to work hard. He feels she'd be an asset to their program."

"An asset to their program . . . ," Laura stammered.

"I'll bet you're really proud," Andrew said with a smile.

"Really proud . . . ," she echoed softly. Laura nodded numbly, not knowing what to say next. *Jess won a scholarship. That's what she was trying to tell me yesterday morning.* Laura had been so impatient, she hadn't even waited to hear the news. Shame suddenly flooded her heart. *I'm a terrible mother. The absolute worst.*

Andrew watched as Laura's eyes filled with tears. *What did I say?* Something had gone terribly wrong, but what? "Laura, is there a problem?"

She nodded, biting her lip. "I, uh . . . I have to go." She stood abruptly, trying to step across him, the jacket dropping down onto the bench below.

"But your son . . . He hasn't even played yet."

"I know, but I have to go."

She looks almost frantic. What did I say?

She made her way down the steps, disappearing into the crowd below. Andrew wasn't sure what he'd done, but somehow he had done it again.

Laura pulled the car up the driveway, relieved to see Nathan's car parked there. *Father, for once let me get this right. Help me to lay down my crazy, foolish pride and show my daughter the kind of love she needs and deserves. Help me to use the right words.* She bounded up the walk to the front door, knocking instead of reaching for her keys. Jessica answered. Nathan stood just behind her.

"We just got here, Mom, I promise," Jess said defensively. Apparently she had prepared herself for an argument.

"I trust you, Jessica, but I really need to talk to you. Do you mind, Nathan?"

"Of course not," he said, reaching for his jacket. "Should I go?"

"No, please stay," she said. "I want you to hear this, too." She stood silently for a moment, trying to decide what to say and how to say it.

"What is it, Mom? Are you gonna stand there all night?" Jess's voice had a sarcastic edge.

"Jess, I'm so sorry." Laura's mind shot back to one of Greg's favorite Sunday school expressions — the twelve words to heal any relationship: *"I am sorry. I was wrong. Please forgive me. I love you."* She would say them all before this conversation ended, no matter how difficult.

Jess looked at her dubiously. "Sorry about what?"

"About getting angry. About the scholarship. It was really wrong of me. Why didn't you tell me?"

"Tell you?"

"About the vocal scholarship."

Jessica's expression changed immediately. "You know?"

"Yes," Laura explained. "I just found out."

"Who told you?"

"Professor Dougherty."

"What? When did you see him?" Jessica looked stunned.

"He was at the game tonight."

"You're kidding. What's he doing — following you?"

"Of course not. It was just a coincidence, but I'm glad he was there. He told me what a great job you did and how proud your vocal instructor is. He told me that you got the scholarship."

"That's what I've been trying to tell you for days, Mom."

"I know that now." Laura reached out to embrace her. "Jessica, I'm so proud of you."

"Right." Her daughter pulled away.

"I am, honey. I really am."

"Well, anyway," Jess said, "it's five hundred dollars. That part should make you happy. I'm going to be less of a burden in the spring than I am now, I guess."

"Jess, please don't talk like that."

"Isn't that what you're thinking?"

"No, it's not what I'm thinking at all."

145

Laura felt a knot in her throat. "What I'm thinking is how very proud I am of you — and how much I would love to have your forgiveness."

Jess shrugged.

"And something else, too," Laura continued. "I love you. I hope you know that."

Her daughter moved toward the door, shaking her head. "Sorry, Mom. Nathan and I were just about to leave. We're going to a nine o'clock movie. Maybe later."

Nathan glanced in Laura's direction, then looked at Jessica. "We don't have to go. This is important. You guys need to talk this out."

"We don't need to talk." Jessica glared at him. Laura couldn't help but see her own reflection in her daughter's countenance.

Nathan shrugged. "Whatever," he said. "But I really don't feel like seeing a movie anymore. I think I'd better go home."

"But —" Jessica never had time to finish her sentence.

Nathan gave her a quick kiss on the cheek and headed to the door. "See you tomorrow," he called out. The door shut behind him.

Jessica's eyes sparkled with anger. "Do you see what you've done? Do you see?"

"What I've done? I just wanted to ask you to forgive me and to tell you that I love you.

I've been so wrong about so many things. I'm so sorry."

"Don't you get it, Mom?" Jessica said angrily. "You ruin everything for me. Everything!" With that, Jessica stormed into her room and slammed the bedroom door behind her.

Unwilling to let it go at that, Laura followed closely behind her, speaking through the door that separated them. "You can shut me out of your room, but you can't shut me out of your life."

Silence.

"I'm going to make mistakes, Jess. Lots of them."

"No kidding." Her daughter's voice sounded muffled.

"I'm human. But I don't ruin everything for you, and I won't stand by and let you say such a thing. You have no idea what it's like to be in my position. Someday, when you have kids . . ."

"That's what all mothers say." Jess opened the door abruptly. "I can't wait until then to understand what makes parents tick. I know that you're so stressed out about everything that you don't even have the time to spend with Kent and me like you used to. You're no fun anymore, Mom."

Laura looked down at the floor, unable to

respond past the growing lump in her throat. "All I can say is I'm sorry, honey. I'm doing my best." A lone tear rolled down her cheek. She brushed it away, embarrassed.

Jessica's face softened slightly. "Mom, I didn't mean to make you cry. I do love you, but I miss things being the way they were. I want life to go back to normal."

"Me, too, honey." Laura reached to give her a hug. "Me, too." They held each other for a few moments before Jess backed away and disappeared into her room.

Laura headed off to the privacy of her own bedroom, her thoughts rolling. She pulled on her flannel pajamas, then reached over to slam the closet door. Greg's suits still hung in the closet, just where he had left them. The time had come to give them away, to put them and the pain of losing her husband behind her. But she couldn't seem to do it. They had remained in the closet this long. They could stay a little longer.

Just looking at Greg's suits reminded Laura of Andrew, of the jacket he so carefully placed across her shoulders earlier this evening. Was it an attempt to reach out to her? To be nice? If so, did she feel ready for that?

Laura tossed herself across the big queen-sized bed for a good, long cry. Her heart hurt so desperately, she hardly knew how to begin mending it. Perhaps it couldn't be mended. The hole left by Greg's death had grown to immense proportions. No one, nothing, could ever fill it. Not now. Not ever.

"Surely I am with you always. . . ." The words from the scripture came to her mind. What brought them there, she could not tell. *"Surely I am with you always. . . ."*

"Who?" she cried out to the stillness of the room. "Who is with me always?" Greg certainly wasn't here. She couldn't wrap herself up in his arms and ask him to make everything all better. She had no one to fill the emptiness she felt. There would never be another human being loving enough to fill that hole, no matter whom she turned to.

What she needed to fill the gaping hole in her life, no human could fill, no mortal man could conjure up. She needed God's assurance. She needed His peace, His strength. She needed Him to move in and take over the loneliness and become the lover of her soul, to be more than just Someone she called out to in her moments of extreme need.

Problem was, she couldn't seem to let go of the pain long enough to allow Him to do that. Maybe she never could.

Andrew drove home in silence, contemplating what had happened at the game. He wanted to call Laura right away, as soon as he arrived home, but he didn't have the courage. What would he say, anyway? Clearly, she hadn't wanted to share her thoughts with him. Maybe she never would.

CHAPTER 14

"I did it again," Andrew said with a sigh.

"Did what?" Regina's eyes were more curious than accusing.

"I blew it." He looked at her for some show of support, hopeful her response wouldn't be negative. He needed a pat on the back, needed someone to tell him he wasn't a total and complete failure.

"Tell me what happened," she said soulfully, as she took a seat. "I don't have to be back behind the counter for fifteen minutes. Will that give you enough time?"

He nodded lamely. "I think so."

"What happened — and be specific."

"I was at the ball game the other night with Laura —"

"You were?" Regina let out a squeal, which caused a lunchroom full of students to turn and look at them. "You asked her out? Well, it's about time. I knew you would. I just knew it."

"No. No, I didn't," he said, trying to quiet her. "I didn't ask her out."

"But you said —"

"I said I was at the ball game with her," he tried to explain. "I didn't say I asked her out."

Regina looked confused, but he plowed ahead. "Anyway, we were sitting there and I don't know what I said, but she just jumped up and ran off."

Regina let out a whistle.

"What?" he asked, avoiding her eyes.

"Must have been pretty awful. What'd you say?"

"That's just it. I didn't say much of anything. I was congratulating her on the music scholarship her daughter just received, and before I knew it, she jumped and ran."

"Maybe her pumpkin was waiting." Regina smiled. "She didn't by any chance drop a shoe when she ran off, did she — 'cause, you know . . ."

"I'm trying to be serious here," he interrupted, getting irritated. "You're supposed to be cheering me up. That's what you do. I come in here and whine, and you cheer me up. That's your job."

"And it's what I'm trying to do, but this time, I think I'm really on your side. Doesn't sound like you did anything wrong. Did that ever occur to you?"

He shrugged.

"Maybe she had something on her mind. Could have just been a bad day. That happens to other people, too, you know. You don't need to take everything so personally."

"I know." He had already considered that possibility. But why had Laura run off at that very moment — just when he brought up Jessica?

"Professor," Regina said, looking at him seriously, "I'm going to give you some sage advice."

He looked into her eyes. If anyone could give advice worth taking, Regina could. She had a depth that seemed undeniable.

"I think it's time to back off and just let nature take its course."

"Let nature take its course? In that case, I might as well forget the whole thing."

"I said, 'back off,' not drop out of the race. There is something you could be doing in the meantime."

"What's that?"

"I'm just wondering. Are you a praying man?" She spoke the words quietly, but with an assurance that seemed to come from deep within.

"A what?" How in the world could he go about answering a question like that?

"A praying man . . ." She said it again, this time looking him right in the eye.

His gaze shifted immediately. It wasn't that he never prayed; it was just that he hadn't for a while — a long while — say five, ten years. "I suppose."

"Well then, why don't you stop all your whining and just get down on those knees of yours," Regina said, "and get busy praying? She'll come around if it's God's plan."

God's plan? "Are you saying I'm supposed to pray for a wife? Is that how desperate I've become?"

"No, of course not." She stood. "You've always been that desperate. You just never knew what to do about it."

"Regina, I never know how to take you. You're kidding, right?"

"No, I'm not. That's how I found my Daniel. I prayed for a godly husband, and before I knew it, Daniel Leal just waltzed into my life. And now that we've already got this woman picked out for you . . ."

"Picked out? Regina, you are too much."

"What are you talking about?" Laura asked the man at the front door. "I paid the electric bill last week."

154

"Better check again, lady," he said, placing a slip of paper in her hand. "According to the office, they never received a payment."

She shook her head in disbelief. "I thought I paid it." *Of course, with everything going on in my life, I could have forgotten.* "Could you wait just a moment while I check?"

"Won't make any difference. I can't take a payment at the door. I'm just here to shut you off."

"But . . ." *This is crazy. I know I paid that bill.*

"You could make a payment online, but they usually take a couple of days to post."

Is he kidding? This house is all electric. We'll freeze to death in here.

"If you want your power turned back on by tomorrow, you could go to one of our payment centers. There's one about five miles from here, on Robinson."

"You look like a very understanding man." She forced a nervous smile. "Would you really do this to us three weeks before Thanksgiving?"

He shrugged, a look of compassion crossing his face. "I just do what they tell me, Ms. Chapman. You understand."

Within minutes the house sat in cold, stony silence. The rattle of the dishwasher no longer hung in the air. The gentle flow of warm air no longer emanated from the vents. The refrigerator ceased to hum. Laura would have missed them all, if she had let herself. But the anger was far too hot in her heart for that. *I know I paid that bill. I remember writing the check.* She thumbed through her checkbook until she came to the one made out to the electric company. *I forgot to mail it. I can't believe it. I've never done anything like that before.*

A surge of emotion raced through her. "It's not fair!" she shouted, though no one was close enough to hear. She leaned against the wall as her knees gave way. Everything seemed to be crumbling around her, and she couldn't do a thing about any of it. Nothing had prepared her for this. Nothing.

She gave herself over to the tears without a moment's guilt. They were long overdue. She had played the role of valiant widow long enough. She couldn't keep the game going any longer. Her heart ached with a fierceness she hadn't known in all of the time since Greg's passing. The full gamut of emotions tore through her. Anger. Pain. Fear. Loneliness.

This can't go on, Lord! I'm asking for Your help, Father — but more than that, I'm asking You to forgive me for not trusting in You.

Increase my faith. Give me courage. I love You, Lord!

CHAPTER 15

Laura shuffled back and forth between the bookstore and home, working until her body passed the point of exhaustion. For over a week, she'd covered both Madeline's hours and her own. It couldn't be avoided. Madeline's bout with the flu required someone to fill her shoes. Laura was the logical candidate. Unfortunately, she'd missed several classes as a result.

The lights might be back on at home, but everything else remained in the dark. Jessica hadn't spoken to her in days. Laura managed to get a few words out of Nathan — something about Jess moving out — but there had been no sign anything like that was actually going to happen.

I'll show her the same patience You've shown me, Lord.

On top of everything, the car broke down. One evening, it just wouldn't start. A dead battery would have been bad enough, but the source of the problem turned out to be an alternator. As usual, when it rained, it poured — at least in her life. But something felt different. Somehow, in the middle of her turmoil, Laura found peace. In the very middle of her storm, she felt anchored.

Her only real regret was being away from school. She had missed two days this week — Tuesday and Thursday. Any more, and she might never get caught up. Her English teacher had been amiable, even offering to e-mail her assignments. Her math home-work would have to wait. And American History — well, there just didn't seem to be much hope that she would ever catch up in that class, so why bother trying?

Andrew sat at the dinner table, listening to his fellow professors drone on about unimportant things. He was up to his ears as they rambled on about economics and politics. To be honest, he didn't give a rip about the latest stock market analysis. He had far more important things on his mind.

Laura Chapman. He couldn't release himself from the image of her wavy hair and silly smirk . . . her soft, smooth skin that carried the bold pink hue of a hot temper when she got riled up . . . her voice, trembling with anger as she spoke. Her "I told you so" smile when she proved him wrong. He missed those things, and so much more. Laura had been absent for the last two classes. With only two weeks before Thanksgiving, he started to worry that she might not come back at all. Truthfully, he missed her. There didn't seem to be any other way to put it. He missed the look of anger in her sparkling eyes. He missed her furrowed brow as she leaned over those unreasonably hard pop quizzes he gave.

For nearly two weeks, he had thought of little but her. When she ran off from the football game that night, she left behind far more than the scent of her perfume. The undeniable lingered in the air. Regina had been right all along. Andrew didn't hate Laura. He liked her — maybe a little too much. What he had grown to feel couldn't be explained without some amount of stammering on his part.

Did he really have room in his heart for someone like Laura Chapman? He hoped so. Perhaps, once the semester ended, he would feel comfortable entering into a relationship. Perhaps.

"Andrew, are you with us?" Sociology professor Mack Brewer, asked.

"Yeah, yeah . . ."

"We were just asking about your position

on yesterday's big story out of Washington. Where do you stand?"

"Oh," he said, trying to focus. "I think it's awful, but I've got faith in our leadership. I'm sure they'll bring us through it all in fine style — if we don't mind hanging in limbo until then."

"What are you talking about?" Mack laughed. "I was asking your opinion on the renovations taking place at the National Art Gallery. What were you talking about?"

"Oh, I, uh . . . ," Andrew stammered. "I'm sorry. I guess I wasn't paying attention."

"Well, that's obvious. But at least we're all aware of your political views!"

Those at the table had a good laugh at Andrew's expense. He turned his attentions back to Laura.

Laura tossed and turned in bed, unable to sleep. She reached across the sheets. In that moment, Laura felt a sudden breeze blow through the room. She gazed at the window. *Surely no one would have opened it in the middle of November.* No, thank goodness, it was closed. But the breeze . . . Where had it come from? She lay, transfixed, watching, wondering. She began to sense an undeniable warmth, a somber satisfaction.

"Surely I am with you always." There was

161

that scripture again. God was taking the time to call out to her, to let her know He was still here. He hadn't gone anywhere. Greg's spot in the bed might be vacant, but she didn't have to be empty.

"Lord, I'm here. Please don't leave me."

"I will never leave you nor forsake you." Another of her favorite scriptures came to mind almost immediately, doing its work to fill the void within. She was not forsaken! God hadn't left her at all. He hadn't been far off. In fact, He was so close, she could almost reach out and touch Him. Laura's heart began to dance within her. She was almost giddy as the words tripped across her tongue, "Thank You, Lord! Thank You!"

Suddenly everything became clear. She had been walking through the valley of the shadow, where the darkness had all but overwhelmed her. But this was a new day. *I'm going to be just fine.* God, the very lover of her soul, was there to remind her of that — and what a sweet reminder!

Emotion gave way to exhaustion and a peace like she hadn't felt in quite some time. Laura fell into a deep, well-deserved sleep.

CHAPTER 16

"Ms. Chapman?"

Laura looked up from the bookshelf into the eyes of Professor Andrew Dougherty. Her heartbeat immediately quickened. *What's he doing here?*

"Professor . . ." She said the word slowly, hesitantly.

He took a step in her direction. "Can you call me Andrew?"

"Mr. Dougherty." She looked the other way. "Is there something I can help you with?"

"I was going to ask you the same thing."

"What do you mean?"

"Well, we've missed you in class this past week, and I thought maybe you'd like your assignments."

Is he actually here on a goodwill mission? "I'm . . . I'm sorry. I've been working a lot of extra hours."

"That's all right. I understand completely.

I just wanted to make sure you weren't staying away because of me."

Interesting remark. Laura looked into his anxious eyes. "No." Had he really been worried about her? Was that possible? "It doesn't have anything to do with you." She straightened the books as she spoke.

"That's good." He sounded relieved. "When you left the game last Saturday night, I felt sure I'd said something wrong. You may recall that I'm pretty good at putting my foot in my mouth."

"I do." She smiled, in spite of herself. "But you didn't do anything wrong this time. To be honest, I didn't know about Jess auditioning for the vocal scholarship. I guess I felt a little left out. I don't know."

"Oh, I'm sorry."

I can't blame him. It's certainly not his fault. "You were just happy for her — which I should have been — but wasn't because we had spent the whole weekend not speaking to each other." Suddenly Laura felt a release to talk, to really talk. For the first time in a long time, it felt great to have someone to share with, even if it was Professor Andrew Dougherty.

Andrew stood, mesmerized, listening to Laura speak. He learned much about her family during those precious minutes — far more than he had counted on. *She's a beautiful woman, inside and out. I can't believe she's taking the time to share all of this with me.*

His heart beat in his ears as he tried to work up the courage to ask her the question on his mind. "Do you get a break anytime soon?"

"I have been here all day, but I haven't gone to lunch yet. Why?"

Why? Because I have plans, if I can just work up the courage to implement them! "There's a deli a couple of doors down," he said nervously. "Have you ever been there?"

"Sure."

"Well, I was hoping you might have time for lunch." *I can't believe the words are coming out of my mouth. Then again, it's not as difficult as I thought it would be.*

She hesitated for what seemed like an eternity. "I, um . . . I'll have to check with Madeline."

He followed her to the front of the store, where her boss's broad smile let him know instantly that she could go. *I can't believe it. I'm actually going out to lunch with Laura Chapman.* Try as he might, he couldn't wipe the silly grin off his face.

"Are you ready?" Laura looked directly

into his eyes and his heart flip-flopped.

Am I ever! "I'm ready." He pulled the door open for her. They stepped out onto the sidewalk, then turned in the direction of the deli.

"Laura, is that you?" Andrew heard the voice, somewhat familiar, and turned. Richard DeHart stood just behind them.

"Dick?" *Talk about lousy timing.*

"I was just coming in to ask you to lunch." DeHart frowned. "Am I too late?"

Andrew jumped in quickly. "We're just headed out — the two of us."

"I'm so sorry." Laura looked from Dick to Andrew and back.

"No problem." Dick reached out to take her arm and a shiver ran down Andrew's spine. "You're both hungry. So am I. What do you say we all go together?"

Andrew's eyes searched out Laura's. He hoped she would say something.

"I don't think —" Laura began.

"You're right," Dick said. "I don't think it's such a bad idea either."

Andrew's pulse quickened. *Dick DeHart is the last man on the planet I'd want to go to lunch with.* He watched out of the corner of his eye as Dick patted Laura's arm. *This guy infuriates me. I should do something about this.* He looked at Laura intently, hoping for some sign of her feelings. Her face looked slightly flushed, but she didn't seem to show the same level of anxiety he felt. Either that, or she was better at hiding it. Worse still, maybe she wanted to go to lunch with Dick DeHart.

"We're just headed down to the deli," Laura said. "I really don't have long, anyway."

"Well then," Dick said, "I'm awfully glad I got here when I did. Talk about great timing."

Yeah. Talk about great timing.

Laura sat at the table between the two men, completely confused and frustrated. Andrew's ears grew redder by the moment. Dick — well, Dick was content to barrel away, pounding Andrew into the ground with his expertise on early American presidents. She could slip away, and they would probably just go right on bickering. She tried, at several points, to enter into their conversation, but they seemed to be talking around her, not to her.

"So," she said finally, "I guess you'll both have to agree to disagree." They'd argued about the difference between the administrations of John Adams and John Quincy Adams for the last ten minutes.

"Are we boring you?" Andrew looked her in the eye.

Boring? Are you kidding me? She was half-asleep already. She shrugged, unwilling to speak her mind. She felt bored, yes, but more irritated than anything — like a third wheel, stuck directly between two flat tires. "I have to get back to work." She stood, relieved to be leaving.

"So soon?" Dick looked at his watch. "We're just getting started."

"Well, I'm sure the two of you will have a lot to talk about once I'm gone." She turned quickly and noticed Jessica, who stood just outside the window.

Oh, dear. Just when I thought things couldn't possibly get any worse.

Andrew stood and pulled out Laura's chair. *She looks frustrated. I don't blame her. This isn't how things were supposed to work out at all.* He had planned a long, lingering lunch over an exhilarating conversation — just between the two of them. *Leave it to Dick DeHart to mess things up.* "Are you sure you have to go?" He gave her his most imploring look.

She turned away from him as she spoke. "I'm already late."

"Would you mind if I stopped by the store

in a few minutes?"

"Whatever."

Is she disinterested or just plain mad?
Laura quickly moved toward the door, taking his hopes with her.

"Looks like it's just the two of us," Dick said with a sly grin.

"Great." Andrew reached to take another drink of his soda. "Just what the doctor ordered."

"Jess, what are you doing down here? Is something wrong? Is Kent in trouble again?"

"Mom, calm down. Kent's fine. Everything's fine. I just wanted to talk to you."

"Talk to me?"

"Yeah, is that so surprising? But it looks like you already have enough people to talk to. You certainly don't need me." She turned abruptly.

"Jessica," Laura said sternly. "This is not what it looks like. Professor Dougherty came by to . . . well, to talk to me about school stuff. He offered to take me to lunch. On the way out the door, we ran into Dick DeHart, and then things got complicated. I just couldn't seem to get rid of him."

"Whatever."

"Jess, stop it. Besides, it's not like I was having a good time." She waved her arms toward the deli to indicate her frustration. "They're both so egotistical and self-serving, they never even saw me."

A faint smile crossed Jessica's lips, the first sign of compromise. She gazed into the window of the deli. Both men seemed to be engrossed in conversation.

"Despite what you might think, I don't like either one of them. I really don't. I wouldn't go out with Dick DeHart under any circumstances, and the professor . . ."

"Yes?" Jessica asked. "What about the professor?"

"Well, he's a nice guy, but . . ."

"Not your type?"

Laura hesitated slightly. "To be honest, I'm not sure what my type is anymore." She gazed through the deli window at Andrew, who looked miserable sitting next to Dick DeHart. *I almost feel sorry for him.*

"Look at them," Jessica said with a smirk. "They're two peas in a pod."

"Aren't they? Let's get out of here and leave them alone." That thought seemed very appealing to Laura.

She and Jessica walked toward the bookstore, laughing and talking about the professor, the tutor, and her daughter's apparent misunderstanding. Laura didn't mind being misunderstood, as long as things were made right again. Within moments, they chatted like youngsters. For the first time in a long time, Laura felt comfortable around her daughter.

They stopped just outside the door of the Bookstop. Jessica's expression changed abruptly. "Mom, there's something I need to talk to you about. That's why I came down here in the first place."

Laura nodded, waiting for her daughter to continue. No one ever wanted to "just talk" anymore, especially not Jess. "What is it, honey?"

"It sounds stupid now, after just blowing up at you. In fact, I've been doing that a lot lately. I can't seem to control my emotions. But that's why I'm here. I, uh . . . I just wanted to apologize."

"For what, honey?"

"Mom," Jessica said tearfully, "I'm just so sorry about everything that's happened this whole semester. I feel like I've ruined everything for you. I should have been more supportive when you told me you wanted to go back to school. You've been through so much these last couple of years, and I couldn't even give you any support at all. I'm selfish. There's no other way to put it." At that, Jessica burst into tears and buried her face in her hands.

"Jess . . ." Laura reached to put her arms around her precious daughter as she spoke. "We've all been through a lot. Ever since your father passed away . . ." The tears filled her eyes as well. "Ever since your father passed away, I've had to become mother and father. Nothing in life prepared me for that. It's hard enough just being Mom. I don't have any idea how to be Dad, too."

"You don't have to be." Jessica lifted her head. "Don't even try. We'll be fine with just you."

The words were freeing. Laura began to weep uncontrollably. Customers passed by. Many gazed at her oddly, but she didn't care.

"I just don't want to get in the way," Jess continued.

"You're not in the way. You never were, and you never will be."

"But I'm such a pain in the neck."

"Yeah," Laura said with a smile. "But aren't we all, sometimes? I mean — I'm a pain, too. Don't you think?"

"Do you really want me to answer that?"

Laura shook her head. "Not really, but we're all grieving, Jessica. And the way you've felt — about the music, about my going back to school, about Nathan, even . . ."

"What about Nathan?"

"I know things have been tense between the two of you," Laura said. "It's pretty clear."

"I don't know what to do about that either. I don't know what to do about anything."

"I think it's time for a fresh start," Laura said firmly. "For all of us. Time to start everything over again."

"How? How do we do that?"

Laura suddenly came to life. "Well, for one thing, I think we need to go back to church on a regular basis. None of this in-and-out stuff."

"I know I could use it," Jess agreed. "My spiritual life has been, well, almost non-existent."

"I'm sure we could all do with a little spiritual help. Besides, I miss being in Sunday school and singing in the choir. Most of all, I long for the closeness I used to feel when we were there together as a family."

"Yeah," Jess responded. "To be honest, I've really missed being in the youth group and all that. Heaven knows, Kent could use it."

"True."

"But, Mom," Jessica said suddenly,

"there's something else I want to do. It's actually the reason I came down here."

"What's that?"

"I want to come to work for you."

"What do you mean?"

Determination etched Jessica's face. "I mean, I want to work some of your hours here at the shop so you can get back into your classes and finish the semester."

"But —"

"I've got it all worked out, Mom. I can give at least two or three hours a day and still keep my schedule at the school. I've even talked to Madeline about it. She's totally cool with the idea. I'll have to miss a couple of history classes, but I'm okay with that. I haven't missed any until recently."

"Madeline wants you to take some of my hours?"

"That's right," her boss said, appearing behind her. "I think it's a great idea, don't you?"

To be honest, Laura didn't know what to think.

CHAPTER 17

"Hey, you!"

Regina's voice rang out, waking Andrew from his lethargy. He had been grading papers — one after another — and welcomed the interruption. Regina stood in the doorway of his classroom, looking as nervous as a cat.

"What's up?"

"Just wanted to come by and let you know something." She walked into the empty room. "I've got news."

"Me, too," he said excitedly. "But you go first. What's up?"

"Nope. You first. Is it something to do with the infamous Ms. Chapman?"

"Maybe."

"Well, come on. Spill the beans. I don't have all day."

"You'd be proud of me," he said with a smile. "We had lunch together."

"You did! You actually did it?"

His gaze shifted to the ground as he spoke. "Sort of."

"Sort of? Tell me."

"I went to the store where she works to talk to her, and there was this deli next door —"

"Good boy, good boy."

"So I asked her if she wanted to go and talk for a while."

"And she said yes?" Regina's voice reflected her glee.

"Uh-huh."

"Andrew, that's great! Then what happened?"

He felt his face fall. "Then DeHart walked up on us."

"Oh no. That weasel."

"Yeah."

"I hope you got rid of him."

Andrew shrugged.

"Don't tell me . . ." Regina stared him down.

"He came to lunch with us."

Regina slapped herself in the head. "I'm about to give up on you, Professor Dougherty. In fact, that's what I came to tell you. You're on your own after today."

"What do you mean?"

She hesitated slightly. "I, uh . . ."

"Spit it out." *She's obviously got something*

on her mind.

"Today was my last day in the lunch-room."

"You quit? Why?"

"Had to," she said. "I'm just too tired."

Don't tell me she's sick. Bad things don't happen to great people like Regina. If anyone deserves a break, she does. "Tell me about it," he said finally. "I mean, if you want to." *I don't want to get too personal.* She stepped toward his desk, half-sitting on the edge. He waited for her explanation.

"It's like this. I–I'm going to have a baby."

He shot out of his seat instantly. "A baby? Are you serious?"

"I'm serious. But my doctor says he wants me off my feet. I'm no spring chicken, you know. Turned forty last month."

"You don't look a day over twenty-nine."

She gave him a thankful smile. "Well, anyway, I just wanted to come over and say good-bye, wanted to make sure you could handle this romance business without me. You're really not very good at it, you know."

"I'm not so sure about that, but I'll do the best I can." He reached over and gave her a playful hug. "Congratulations, Regina." He felt a lump in his throat. "I'm very happy for you. Please tell Daniel for me."

"I will." She returned the hug. "In fact,

he's waiting for me in the car. We're both tickled pink." She paused. "Better make that blue. He's holding out for a boy."

Laura entered the American History classroom, struggling with her emotions. She wanted desperately to be here and yet felt terrified at the same time. As she came through the door, she saw Andrew with his arms wrapped around the lady from the lunchroom in a warm embrace. Laura stood, transfixed. She couldn't seem to move forward. She didn't want to go backward.

"I'll see you later, Andrew," the woman said, passing by her at the doorway. Laura noticed the woman stared at her. A twinge of jealousy shot through her, though she wasn't sure why.

"Ms. Chapman." She looked up into the eyes of Andrew Dougherty, amazed at the twinkle she found there. "You're back?"

"I'm back," she said, trying not to let her emotions show. "I've got to get through these last few weeks somehow."

He smiled a warm, inviting smile. "It's going to be just fine, and I'm going to help you."

Andrew's heart pounded so hard, he could

scarcely breathe. Laura had returned. His trip to the store must have made the difference. He looked at her inquisitively. Was she here because she really wanted to be? Did it have anything to do with him at all?

"My daughter is going to miss class today," Laura explained. "She's taken some of my hours at the bookstore."

Ah. So, Jessica made all of this possible. Well, thank goodness for Jessica! "I'll be glad to send her work home with you."

"Thank you — for everything." She offered up a smile, one that warmed him to his toes.

Andrew fought to keep his composure. He wanted to know what made her tick, what gave her such tenacity. He wanted to take back everything he had ever thought about her being lazy. Laura Chapman had turned out to be one of the hardest workers he'd ever come across in his years as a teacher. Should he tell her, give her some sort of confirmation she would make it?

Andrew watched as she sat at her desk and pulled open the textbook. He turned his gaze to the board, where he wrote questions from today's lesson, then turned slightly to see if she had watched him. No, her head remained buried in the book. She seemed to be lost in her own world.

She probably thinks I'm going to give another pop quiz. Well, not today. No, he would take it easy on his students for a change. For some reason, he felt like a new man, invigorated, alive. As the rest of the students entered and took their seats, he made a silent pact with himself to give them a break.

"Welcome, everyone." He turned to face the class. "I trust you all managed to get through the work sheet I gave you when we met last."

A slight rumble went up from the students, who reached for their papers.

"Well, let's forget all about that and take a look at something else." They looked up at him, obviously startled.

"You mean we don't have to turn them in?" one of the boys asked.

"Not this time."

A look of relief flooded several faces. Still others looked puzzled. "Are you feeling all right, Professor Dougherty?" one of the girls asked.

"Never better." He turned his attention to an enlightening discussion on the Industrial Revolution, trying to remain focused. The students chimed in, creating a lively discussion. From the front of the room he kept a watchful eye on Laura. What was she thinking? Had he said anything to offend her?

No, she appeared to be smiling, enjoying the conversation as much as the others. All through the class, Andrew couldn't seem to take his eyes off of Laura. She seemed different, somehow — more peaceful than before. The angry edge was gone, replaced with the closest thing to happiness he had observed in quite awhile.

His heart continued to race as he concluded the class. Andrew hoped for a way to keep Laura after class, to ask her . . .

What he really wanted to do was ask her out, but he couldn't even say the words to himself. A date. He wanted a real date with her. But would she? Maybe after the semester ended? She certainly hadn't shown interest in him at the deli the other day. Then again, that was Dick DeHart's fault. He had ruined the afternoon entirely.

Andrew dismissed the class, waiting to see if she would linger behind the group. Their eyes met for a brief moment. He turned his gaze to the papers on the desk, embarrassed that she had caught him looking at her. He looked back up again, disappointed to find she had slipped out of her seat and was headed toward the door.

"Ms. Chapman?"

"Yes?" She turned, looking at him.

"I wonder . . . I wonder if you could stay

after class for a few moments," he said, feeling his hands begin to shake.

"Why?"

"Well, I, uh . . ." The other students disappeared down the hallway, leaving them alone.

"I want to tell you how happy I am to see you. I'm glad you're back."

She looked startled. "You are?"

"Certainly. Haven't you figured that out yet?" He fought to continue. "I enjoy your company, Ms. Chapman." Andrew searched her eyes for a response.

Her face flushed as she whispered hoarsely, "Call me Laura."

"Laura." His hands shook uncontrollably now. "That's why I wanted to take you to lunch the other day. I'm so sorry about the way everything turned out."

"Me, too."

"I wanted to spend some time alone with you, to get to know you. I wanted to make up for the time I've spent poking fun at you or making assumptions."

"It's all in the past. I hope you can forgive me for the day we met."

He smiled, remembering. "Done." He paused slightly. "Do you still think I'm so tough?"

"In a good way. Most of these kids need a

little push. I know you've made me a better student."

"I have?"

"If nothing else, you motivated me, made me want to be the best I could be. That's what every good teacher strives to do, right?"

"Right." Andrew stared at her in disbelief. *She's so giving.* "Look," he said, feeling strength well up in him, "I've been trying to work up the courage to ask you something."

She looked up, their gazes locking. "What is that?"

"This probably isn't the right time or place. . . ." He looked toward the door. Any moment now, students from his next class would be arriving. It was now or never. "I've been wanting to ask you out on a date. A real date. Just the two of us."

"Are you serious?"

"Never more serious."

She bit her lip before responding. "I'm not sure if I'm ready for that yet."

His heart twisted inside him as he took her hand. "Will you let me know when you are? I don't want to rush you, but I'd love to spend some time getting to know you better."

She nodded silently. "I'll do that."

His heart swelled. "That would be great."

Just then, two students barreled through the door, laughing at one another. Laura quickly pulled her hand from his and moved away. "I really need to get to work. Jess has been so good to cover for me, but I'm sure she's ready for a break." She smiled, then left the room in a hurry.

Andrew turned toward the board, erasing the notes from the last class. His heart soared as he contemplated her words. "Andrew Dougherty," he whispered, "I do believe you're making progress."

CHAPTER 18

"Kent? Jessica? Are you guys ready?" Laura called out in an attempt to rush them. "We're going to be late to church." Something about the words reminded her of when they were children. Many a Sunday morning had been spent looking for missing shoes or socks or arguing over appropriate church attire. She and Greg had always managed to get them out the door and to church in time for Sunday school.

Kent appeared at the top of the stairs, still in his pajama pants and T-shirt. He stretched, letting out a loud, rehearsed moan. "Mornin'."

"What are you doing, Kent? I told you to get ready nearly an hour ago."

"I fell back asleep," he said with a yawn. "Just go on without me."

"Go to church without you? But —"

"Aw, give me a break, Mom. I've had a tough week at school. I'm beat."

Laura felt the disappointment deeply. *I wanted this to be a family affair. Well, at least Jessica will go with me.*

"Jess?" She called up the stairs. Her daughter appeared, dressed in a trendy blouse and skirt.

"You look great."

"Thanks." Jessica smiled. "So do you."

"Did you say Nathan wanted to sit with us this morning?"

"He's meeting us there. He always rides with his parents, anyway." She pulled the door shut behind them, and they headed out to the car. The air outside felt crisp and cold. Laura shivered, pulling her jacket tightly around herself. Doing so reminded her of the night at the football game when Andrew pulled his jacket over her shoulders to keep her warm. *Andrew.* Thinking of him brought an unexpected smile. *Is it possible I'm beginning to have feelings for this man?*

"It's almost Thanksgiving." Jessica interrupted her thoughts as they climbed into the car. "Can you believe it? It seems like the semester just started."

"Seems more like an eternity to me, but I'm happy the holidays are coming. It means I'm one step closer to being done with my first leg of the journey."

"You've done a great job, Mom. I'm really

proud of you."

Laura felt her heart swell. "I never thought I'd hear those words — not from you, anyway."

"Well, just like you've been saying — today's a new day."

They drove to the church, chatting about everything from Christmas gifts to Thanksgiving dinner. It was a truly wonderful trip.

Andrew changed the channels on the TV, frustrated. *Church services.* He certainly wasn't interested in any of those . . . or was he? One, in particular, caught his eye. It was a room full of people, singing, worshiping. They seemed to be happy, in an odd sort of way.

"What phonies. Like anyone could be that happy in church."

And yet, he couldn't seem to change the channel. Something about those people held him captivated — something in their expression intrigued him. They didn't look like they were faking anything. In fact, they looked perfectly natural, genuinely comfortable.

"Comfortable in church. Now that's something I've never felt." It wasn't like Andrew had never been to church. He had been raised in one. His strict mother had pulled him out of the arms of his agnostic father every Sunday until Andrew turned about twelve or thirteen. That's when he rebelled — started staying home with his dad for one-on-one conversations about the things that really interested him — explorers, navigators, maps, and so much more. That's where the fun had been. He certainly never experienced any joy sitting in a pew.

Joy. There seemed to be so little of it in his life. His passion for teaching brought him joy, but not the kind that really lasted. Those people on the television looked like they had something that superceded what he felt in front of the classroom. Their joy seemed to come from something inside, something he couldn't quite understand. "I don't get it," he whispered, "but I'd sure like to figure it out."

He watched as the pastor brought the congregation to laughter with a joke about children. "No, I never went to a church like that." He spoke to the empty room. "But maybe someday I will."

"Turn with me to Colossians, chapter three," the pastor said. "Verses twelve through fourteen."

Laura turned through her worn Bible until she found the passage. She had always loved this one, but somehow, in the middle of things, she had simply forgotten about it.

The pastor's voice rang out against the silence. " 'Therefore, as God's chosen people, holy and dearly loved, clothe yourselves with compassion, kindness, humility, gentleness and patience.' "

Kindness? Patience? Laura had shown little of these traits over the last several months, in spite of her good intentions.

" 'Bear with each other,' " the pastor continued, " 'and forgive whatever grievances you may have against one another. Forgive as the Lord forgave you.' "

She had forgiven everyone, hadn't she? After all, she excused Jessica for giving her the cold shoulder. She pardoned Kent for complicating their already complicated lives with his shenanigans. She had forgiven Greg . . . Wait a minute! Greg hadn't done anything wrong. Why should she have to forgive him? Could she possibly be holding him in unforgiveness — after all this time?

The pastor continued on, oblivious to her inner turmoil: " 'And over all these virtues put on love, which binds them all together in perfect unity.' "

Love. She and Greg had been in love — the kind that surpassed romance. The kind that could have lasted forever — at least

189

that's what she always thought. Gentle tears began to course down Laura's cheeks. She reached for a tissue but found none. Jessica quickly handed her one, then reached out to touch her arm.

"It's all right, Mom," she whispered, eyes glistening. "I know how you feel."

The pastor went on to talk about the steps to mend broken relationships. Laura took notes, scribbling down as many words as she could on the back of an offering envelope. Jess handed her the church bulletin, pointing to a blank spot on the back. "There you go, Mom," she whispered.

Laura reached to pat her hand, a gesture of thanks. *Lord, thank You so much for sending Jessica with me. I love spending time with her.* She paused from her note-taking, content to sit with her hand wrapped around her daughter's. She could go on sitting like this forever.

The service ended some time later, but Laura couldn't seem to pull herself from the sanctuary. Even after most of the others left, she remained. She slowly made her way up to the front, a place she had often visited as a child. Funny how the altar still cried out to her. Jess had disappeared to the foyer with Nathan, so Laura took advantage of the situation by kneeling for a few moments alone.

"Lord, I'm here," she whispered. "I made it. And I'm back to stay this time. I'm not going anywhere." She felt the presence of God overwhelm her. "How did I stay away so long?" She spent a few more minutes opening up her heart to her Father. How wonderful it felt to be back in this place, the very place Greg had loved so much.

"Greg." No sooner did she speak his name than she realized what she must do. "I have to forgive him, Lord. Help me."

Her daughter appeared behind her. "Mom, is there anything I can do?"

"No, Jess." She looked up with a smile, dabbing at her eyes.

"I'm worried about you."

"No need to worry. This is a good thing."

"Are you sure?"

Laura nodded. "Yes, but I'm not sure I can explain what I'm feeling right now."

"Could you try?" Jessica knelt down beside her.

Laura took her hand and clutched it tightly. "When your father died . . ." That was all she got out before the tears came again.

"Tell me, Mom."

Laura took a deep breath. "When your

father died, I blamed God. I didn't realize it until months later. I was so angry with Him that I never wanted to come back into a church again. In fact, I even told Him that."

"You did?"

"Yes, but it was wrong of me. I knew that, after awhile. That day — when you came up to the store — I realized then that I was also angry at you kids."

"At us? Why? What did we do?"

"It wasn't anything you did, exactly. The situation I found myself in had reached a crisis point. Don't you see? I've been completely responsible for the two of you with no one to help me. Since I had locked God out, I sure couldn't look to Him for help. That left me on my own. But that day you came up to the store, God began to show me this."

"Really?"

"Yes. He showed me that unforgiveness is like a prison. It holds us in its grip until we can't breathe. Eventually we become so bitter, we're no fun to be around. I don't want to be like that!" At that, Laura began to cry unashamed. "Can you ever forgive me, Jess? I'm so sorry about everything!"

"Mom, of course I do, and I know Kent will, too. But you have to forgive us, too. We haven't exactly made things easier." They embraced for what seemed like an eternity.

"There's something else," Laura said finally. "And this is the worst part. I didn't realize it until just this morning. I really didn't."

"What, Mom?"

"I've been angry with your father." She spoke through the tears. "I've been so angry with him, I couldn't think straight. He left me. He abandoned me."

Jessica held her tightly. "I do understand, Mom. More than you know. I've been mad at Daddy, too. I've been so mad, sometimes I fight with him in my dreams."

"You what?"

"I dream about him," Jessica explained, "and we always end up fighting. I argue and argue but never seem to win. He always wins. But then I wake up and realize what's happened — that it's just a dream — and try to put it out of my mind. But the dreams don't go away."

"Jess, I never knew."

"I know," she said sadly. "I never told you. I just wake up in a bad mood and take it out on you and Kent. I have a feeling things are going to be better after today, don't you?"

"It felt really good to go back to church." Laura smiled through the tears. "I mean, it was hard — seeing all of those women sitting there with their husbands beside them, but it still felt wonderful."

"I thought so, too. I missed having Daddy next to me, trying to sing bass."

"He had a terrible voice," Laura said with a smile. "Do you remember?"

Jess laughed. "How could I forget?"

He hadn't been the best singer in the world, but he had certainly made up for it by being the best husband.

"Jess, would you pray with me before we leave?"

"Here?" Her daughter looked around. "Out loud?"

Laura nodded. "If you don't mind."

Jessica began to pray aloud, hesitantly at first, then gaining strength as she went. Her prayer was passionate, heartfelt. As she continued on, Laura's heart swelled with joy inside her. She had truly come home.

Andrew paced back and forth across his tiny living room, the words from the television still on his mind. Something the TV pastor had said intrigued him. He couldn't seem to shake it: " 'Be transformed by the renewing of your mind . . . ,' " or something like that.

"Transforming your mind." He repeated

the words. Andrew understood the concept of strengthening his mind by gaining knowledge, of bettering himself. That's why he had spent so many years in college, and why he felt driven to teach.

But this idea of transforming his mind . . . Now that was certainly something new, something to think about.

"Does he mean I should gain more knowledge?" he asked, pacing across the room. "Or is there something more?"

He headed to the computer, rapidly signing online. "Surely there's got to be some sort of Bible online I can read," he spoke aloud. "I'll get this figured out."

Before he knew it, three hours had passed. Bleary-eyed, Andrew reached to shut down the computer, his mind reeling. If the scriptures he'd read were true, bettering his mind didn't have anything to do with education.

It had everything to do with inspiration.

"I'm sorry . . . what did you say?" Laura felt sure she had heard the voice on the other end of the phone correctly, but she didn't want to believe it.

"This is Officer Meyer with the Harris County Sheriff's Office. Your son was in an accident on Interstate 45 about half an hour ago and has been taken to Northwest Hospital."

Please, God, no! "I'm on my way." Laura suddenly felt faint. She hung the phone up, trembling as she called, "Jess!"

Her daughter appeared quickly, a look of fear crossing her face when she saw her mother. "What is it?"

"It's Kent."

"What about him?"

"He's been in an accident."

"What? What happened?"

"I don't know. They didn't say."

"Where is he?"

"Northwest. Can you drive?"

Jessica nodded, taking the keys from her hand. "Of course. You just get whatever you think you'll need. Do you have his insurance card?"

Laura nodded lamely, letting her daughter take charge. If nothing else, it felt good to have someone else in control — at least for the moment.

Laura felt numb as they made their way outside.

"When we get there, I'm going to let you off at the door," Jess explained as they got into the car. "Then I'm going to park. Getting a parking space at Northwest isn't easy. Did they say where to go? Is he in the

196

Emergency Room, or have they moved him?"

"I — I don't know." Laura tried to speak over the lump in her throat. "I forgot to ask."

"Well, we'll start there. Don't worry, Mom. I know he's going to be all right."

Laura nodded numbly, trying to collect her thoughts. She hadn't asked for any information at all. *I don't know who was driving, how many other people were injured, or if Kent was badly hurt. I only know that he needs me — and quickly.* The ride to the hospital seemed to take forever. *Are they ever going to finish these interstates? This construction is ludicrous.* "Take the back way."

Jessica followed her instructions, and they quickly reached the hospital. "Just stay calm, Mom. Don't let Kent see you upset. You need to be strong."

Laura didn't feel strong. She felt completely unprepared to face whatever lay on the other side of that door, but she had to put her best foot forward — for Kent's sake.

"I'm Mrs. Chapman," she said to the first official-looking person she came in contact with.

The elderly woman nodded compassionately. "They've taken your son into surgery."

"Surgery?"

"Yes, ma'am. The doctor will tell you all about it when they're done. In the meantime, a police officer is here, waiting to speak with you." She pointed to her right.

Laura made her way to the officer, who sat filling out papers. "I'm Laura Chapman. Could you tell me what happened to my son?"

"Officer Meyer." He stuck his hand out to grasp hers. "Nice to meet you. I'm sorry it has to be under these circumstances."

"Please tell me something."

"Your son was in a major collision on I-45," the officer explained. "Apparently, a friend of his was driving under the influence."

Driving under the influence? "Who? What friend?"

"We're still trying to determine that, ma'am. He came in without any ID, and your son was in a state of shock — unable to identify him. The doctor will give you details when he comes out of the operating room, but I can tell you, Kent's in pretty bad shape. A paramedic mentioned the possibility of internal bleeding. We had to Life Flight him here."

Laura spoke over the knot in her throat. "How did you know to call me?"

"Kent had his permit in his wallet," the deputy explained. "Wish the other boy had."

"But you're sure Kent wasn't driving?"

"We're sure. The other boy is pretty cut up — took some damage from the steering wheel and the air bag. He didn't have a seat belt on."

"Oh no . . ."

"Would you please come and have a look at him for us? We're really hoping you can help identify him."

Laura followed him to the room where the boy lay unconscious, hooked up to various machines. He was almost unrecognizable — the cuts on his face and head were bandaged, covering much of his face.

"I know him," she whispered. "His mother is a good friend. His name is Josh. Josh Peterson. He's just a kid. . . ."

"An intoxicated kid who lost control of his car and hit the railing on the interstate. He managed to hit two other cars."

"Did he hurt anyone else?"

The officer shook his head. "No, not this time. But we need some information on Josh. Do you have a phone number? We'll need to contact his parents."

"Is he going to be alright?" She quickly

scribbled the number on a piece of paper and handed it to him.

"He looks bad, but the doctors say his wounds are superficial. If I were you, I'd focus on Kent. In fact, I'll ask an aide to walk you down to the surgical waiting area so you're there when they finish with him."

Laura followed the aide down the long hallway, a prayer on her lips the entire way. *Father, I'm asking You to guard the surgeon's hands as he operates on Kent. He needs Your healing, Lord. Help him. Help Josh. Help us all.*

Laura collapsed numbly into a chair in the waiting area. Jessica arrived, breathless, a few minutes later.

"That parking garage is a madhouse," she said, panting. "What did they say? Is he here?"

"They've taken him to surgery," Laura said, giving way to the tears.

"Surgery? Why? What's wrong with him?"

"I don't really know. The doctor will tell us when he comes out. I guess we'll just have to wait and see."

"Wait and see?"

"There is something you can do, Jess," Laura said, gathering her strength. "I need you to call Grandma, and I need you to give the Petersons a call, just to make sure they got the message."

"What message? What do the Petersons have to do with this?"

"Josh was driving the car. He was . . . the policeman said he was driving under the influence."

"No!"

"That's what he said. But please, just make the calls. Don't tell them that part — at least not yet. Just make sure they come. I've got to go in and see Josh again, make sure he's okay. I feel like someone needs to be in there with him." She reached out to embrace her daughter, squeezing her tightly.

"I know everything will be okay. We'll get through this. If God is for us —"

"Who can be against us," Laura finished the scripture with her daughter's hand tightly clutched in her own.

Chapter 19

Andrew stood in his classroom, silent after a long day's teaching. He'd just received the news that Laura's son had been in an accident, and Andrew found himself torn. *Surely I should do something, but what? Send flowers? Drop off a card?*

Did he dare go up to the hospital? Would that be too forward? Andrew paced nervously to the board, erasing all that had been written there during the last class.

I should go. I should. It didn't take much more to convince himself.

"Mom? Are you all right?"

Laura awoke suddenly, fearfully, looking toward the hospital bed. An immediate fear gripped her. "Kent?"

"No, Mom. It's me, Jess. I didn't realize you were sleeping. I didn't mean to wake you."

Laura's nerves calmed immediately. She

turned to face her daughter, who stood in the doorway. Just the tone of Jessica's voice soothed her. "Oh, that's okay. I shouldn't have been dozing."

"Why not? If anyone deserves to rest, you do. You've been shut up in this hospital room for three days now."

That was true, though Laura wouldn't have had it any other way. How could she possibly leave Kent's side? He was still not out of danger. Though the surgery to remove his lacerated spleen went well, there was still the broken arm to contend with. The orthopedist insisted Kent needed to stabilize before he could surgically repair the fracture. That surgery had taken place just this morning. It didn't matter how long any of this took. Laura would stay regardless of how much it taxed her.

"He's been sleeping for hours." She yawned loudly.

"You need a break," Jess said. "I thought I'd stay awhile."

"I could stand some food." Laura felt a surge of strength rise within her. "Maybe I could go down to the cafeteria. Have you eaten?"

"Yep. Stopped off at the cafeteria after class."

Laura's heart twisted within her as she

thought about the classes she had missed. "How was school? Were you able to make it to all of your classes?"

"Yep. Everything at school is fine." Her daughter reached into her backpack to pull out some papers. "These are from Dougherty. He said he hopes to see you soon — whatever that means."

"Did you tell him?" Laura didn't know why it seemed important that he know . . . but it did, somehow.

"Yeah. He looked pretty shook up but said not to worry about class, that everything would be fine. He knows you're a good student."

"Humph. Don't know about that."

"Well, anyway. I told him you were shut up here with little to do, so he sent some work over. Hope that's all right."

"Sure. Whatever. I need something to pass the time." While she had been intent on staying by Kent's side, there had been little to do but watch TV, chat with the doctor about his condition, and pray. Laura had done a lot of praying over the last few days.

"Anything else?"

"I talked to Madeline. She also said not to worry — you've still got a few sick days coming to you."

"Yeah, but the day after Thanksgiving is

the busiest day of the year," Laura said nervously. "I know she'll need me then."

"Let's just take this one day at a time, Mom."

Laura nodded. She was right. Besides, Laura couldn't do anything about it, anyway. "Anything else going on that I need to know about?"

"Nope."

"Well, in that case, I'd love to get some coffee and something to nibble on." Laura looked around the room, still feeling a little unsure about leaving.

"Go on . . . ," Jess urged.

"I'll be in the cafeteria if anyone needs me. And I may stop by the chapel for a few minutes." *I've meant to do that for days.*

Jessica gave a nod. "Go on, Mom. Get out of here for a while. I'll hold down the fort."

Laura turned to leave the room. As much as she hated to go, she felt she had to get out for at least a few minutes. She made her way down to the cafeteria, finding a spot at a table where she could be alone to drink her coffee and nibble on a banana. She then headed back toward the room, walking slowly through the now-familiar halls of the first floor of Northwest Hospital.

Laura paused at the chapel door. *I should go inside.* To be honest, she had avoided it for days, though she couldn't put her finger on a legitimate reason. A hospital chapel shouldn't frighten her. She tiptoed into the empty room, making her way to the altar where a Bible lay open.

Quietly she sank to her knees, though doing so felt a little awkward. Once there, the tears began to flow. She hadn't planned them. They just seemed to erupt from a deep place within her — a place that needed comforting. Where the words came from, she wasn't quite sure, but they began to flow, too.

"Father, do You ever get tired of hearing how much I need You? If it's a lack of faith on my part, then give me more. I need You more than ever. I don't know how to make it through this alone. I can't do it on my own. Take care of Kent, Father. Heal him. Mend his broken heart so he can let go of the anger he's been holding onto. Lord, I pray that Your work would be complete, not just in Kent, but in me. Take away the things in my life that aren't pleasing to You. Make me the woman you want me to be. Help me to know how to show Your love to the people You've placed in my life."

Laura poured her heart out to the Lord, begging Him to spare her son, and asking Him to forgive her for every conceivable thing she could think of. Somehow, at the end of it all, she felt the burden lift.

Andrew Dougherty stood outside the chapel of Northwest Hospital, listening. Jessica had said he might find Laura here, though he was completely unprepared for the way he found her. She was praying, actually praying out loud, and on her knees.

As a child, he had spent many hours on his own knees — punishment from a stern mother who used prayer as a means to an end: to bring him to repentance for his thoroughly wicked deeds. He had spent more time daydreaming than praying back then, but if he had known prayer could be this simple, he might have tried it.

Andrew had never heard anyone pray like this before. Laura's words were genuine, heartfelt. They spoke volumes. He felt like a traitor as he strained to hear each and every word. They weren't his to hear, and yet somehow they sounded as comfortable and comforting as anything he had heard in a long, long time.

"Be transformed by the renewing of your mind. . . ." The scripture ran through his head once again. For the first time in his life, he began to understand just how possible that could be. *Lord, is it really that*

easy? Do I just talk to You like she's doing? Can it be that simple?

Relief flooded his soul. Perhaps this wasn't something he would have to earn. Maybe it wouldn't require a huge amount of study on his part. Perhaps all he had to do was just believe.

The sound of a man's cough at the chapel door roused Laura from the altar. She wiped at her eyes and tried to get control of her emotions. She didn't want anyone to see her like this, even a stranger. Laura reached for a tissue but couldn't seem to find one.

"Are you looking for this?" A man pressed a tissue into her hand.

She didn't dare look up. "Thank you."

"I hoped I'd find you here," he said softly.

Laura suddenly recognized the voice. She turned, finding herself face-to-face with Andrew Dougherty. Instinctively, she reached out to take the hand he offered, letting him pull her to a standing position. His arm slipped around her shoulder in a warm, sincere hug. There was nothing uncomfortable or awkward about it.

Wrapped in his embrace, she felt completely free to let the tears flow. Her face found its way to his shoulder, where she buried it, sobbing uncontrollably. He wrapped both arms around her, whispering gentle words of reassurance. "It's going to be okay." His fingers brushed against her hair and Laura found comfort in his touch. He had come at just the right moment. She needed someone to be there just then. She'd longed for it for quite some time, though she hadn't realized just how much.

But Andrew Dougherty?

Funny. His touch was tender, loving, nothing like she would have expected. He caressed her hair with his fingertips, pausing to brush it from her eyes. None of this made sense, and yet she couldn't deny the feeling of peace and satisfaction she felt wrapped up in his arms. The whole thing felt perfectly natural. It felt good.

Too good.

After a few moments she pulled away and forced her gaze in another direction. Embarrassment filled her. "I'm so sorry. I don't know what came over me."

"Please, don't be sorry." Andrew felt his heart swell. "I wanted to be here for you. It's the least I can do."

Laura Chapman had felt good in his arms. So very good. The scent of her shampoo lingered, dizzying him. It had been years since he had been close enough to a woman to smell that. His fingers had run through her hair with a mind of their own. That lustrous hair of hers had always been a temptation for him. Andrew's arms ached to reach for her again, to wrap her up into them and whisper comforting words to her. It felt so right.

Andrew could no longer deny his feelings for Laura Chapman. He desired to know her as a friend and as much more.

He spoke softly. "That prayer of yours . . ."

"You heard me pray?"

"Yes. That prayer was beautiful. I haven't heard anything so incredible since I was a kid in Sunday school."

"You're making fun of me."

"No, I'm not." He meant every word of it.

"You were a Sunday school kid? That's hard to believe."

"I know, but it's true," Andrew said with a sigh. "Somewhere along the way, I turned my back on God. When I got to my teens, I guess. I remember accepting Christ at an altar when I was nine. It seems like a lifetime ago. But I never learned to pray like that. Never."

"I'm just remembering how to do it, myself. Turns out it's pretty simple. You talk, He listens. He talks, you listen."

Andrew shook his head in disbelief. "In the academic world, everything has to be earned — every grade, every promotion. Everything. Nothing comes easy."

"Prayer should."

"I can see that. Now. I'm not sure what I've believed about God since my days in college. It's like I put Him away on a shelf and forgot about Him."

"What about now? What do you believe?"

"I believe . . ." Here Andrew hesitated. He wasn't completely sure how to go about saying what was in his heart. "For years, I have been frustrated. So many things have happened to make me give up on God and on people — mostly women."

"Women? Why?"

How could he begin to explain why? "I was engaged once, but something happened on the way to the church."

"She broke your heart?"

Andrew nodded lamely. "Yeah."

"I figured as much."

"What do you mean?"

"It wasn't so hard to figure out that someone must have hurt you at some point along the way. Is that why you're so angry with God?"

"What do you mean? Who said anything about that?"

"Isn't that what this is all about?" Laura asked. "I know I've had to struggle with that. Ever since Greg died, I've been so mad at God, I hardly knew how to function. But admitting it is half of the battle. It gets easier after that."

Andrew laughed and shook his head in disbelief. "You are something else. Just about the time I think I've got you figured out, I find out that there's so much more."

"I'm not such a bad person," Laura said with a smile. She looked down at her watch and gasped. "I have to get back up to the room. Jessica is up there alone with Kent, and I need to be with her."

"Would you mind if I came along?" He almost dreaded her answer.

To his relief, she shrugged. "No, come if you like. I'm sure Jess would be glad to see you."

He walked beside her, chatting all the way. What he wanted to do — what he longed to do — was to pull her close to him and tell her everything would be all right. Would she think him awful if he reached for her now? No, that wouldn't be the appropriate thing to do. What had happened in the chapel had been perfectly natural, perfectly comfortable, but anything more would spoil an otherwise perfect moment.

Andrew continued to ramble on about everything from the weather to his latest history quiz. Truth be told, he was so nervous, much of what he said didn't make a lot of sense. Not that she seemed to notice. Laura's mind appeared to be a million miles away.

Chapter 20

"Hello there."

Laura looked up as Andrew peeked in the door of the hospital room. Her heart skipped a beat as their eyes met. His visit yesterday had been unexpected, but today she had secretly hoped he would come. He stood in the doorway, clearly hesitant.

Laura laid down the magazine she had been reading. "Well, hello."

"How's our patient today?" He turned his gaze toward the bed, where Kent lay sleeping.

"Better. But they are keeping him pretty sedated. He's been sleeping most of the day."

"What about you?" Andrew took a couple of steps into the room. "Have you had any sleep?"

She shrugged. "A little." An embarrassing yawn worked its way to her lips.

He pulled a small bouquet of flowers from

behind his back. "I thought these might cheer you up."

Yellow roses. I love yellow roses. "Are they for me or Kent?" She suddenly felt like a shy schoolgirl.

"They're for you." He handed them to her. She clutched them tightly, suddenly unable to breathe correctly.

"I actually have something else for him, when he wakes up, that is." Andrew reached inside his coat and pulled a small package from the pocket.

"What is that?"

"It's a CD. Dizzy Gillespie. He's a trumpet player."

"Dizzy Gillespie? How in the world did you know —"

He laid it on the bedside table. "The football game, remember? After you left, I stayed to watch Kent play. I don't know much about trumpets or trumpet players, but he looked like he knew his stuff."

Laura nodded, stunned. She couldn't seem to get past the fact that Andrew had handed her three yellow roses, which she still held tightly. They smelled incredible. She ran her finger over one of the blossoms. "And I'm sure he'll love it. It was very thoughtful of you." *Very thoughtful.*

"No problem. I enjoyed shopping for it.

215

I'm not much of a contemporary music person, but I love to browse through the old stuff." Kent stirred slightly in the bed. "Sorry, I guess I'm too loud," Andrew whispered.

"No, trust me. Nothing could wake him." Laura stood and carried the roses toward the bathroom. "I need to get these in some water." As she crossed in front of Andrew, their eyes met. He held her captive for a moment with his smile, and her heartbeat accelerated slightly. Laura glanced at the ground nervously, then chose to keep walking.

"I'll just be a minute," she said, then entered the bathroom. She quickly turned on the tap water with one hand, unwrapping the roses with the other. She glanced around for something to put them in. The only thing she could find was a small glass. "This will have to do." She broke the stems off at the bottom, then placed them in the glass, which she filled with water. They leaned a little too far to the right.

"I think I'll put them on the windowsill." She walked past him once again, feeling his eyes on her hair. *Why am I so nervous? It's not like I've never been alone in a room with him.*

"I was hoping you might be able to take a

little break."

"A break?"

"Yeah. I thought we might grab something to eat in the cafeteria."

"I don't know." Laura looked nervously at Kent, who lay in a sound sleep. "He might need me." She yawned again. "I am hungry. And I haven't been out of this room all day. Maybe I could just stop by the nurses' station and tell them where I'll be."

"Sounds good."

She went to Kent's bedside, stopping to brush a kiss across his forehead. Her heart twisted as she gazed at him. *I won't do it. I won't get down about this. The doctors say he's going to be fine. I can be strong. I will be strong.*

She turned to face Andrew, immediately relieved by his presence. "I think I'm ready now."

He smiled and led the way out of the door.

Andrew sat across the table from Laura in the hospital cafeteria, mesmerized by her conversation. "And then what happened?"

"Then I told the kids that they were never allowed to eat peanut butter and jelly again — at least, not in the living room!" She chuckled then sighed deeply. "It feels good to laugh. It really does."

217

"You've got a great laugh."

"What do you mean?"

"Oh, come on. You know. Some women have those really high-pitched, annoying laughs. They hurt your ears. And some have that terrible snorting laugh. That's the worst."

"And I'm neither of those?"

"No, you have the perfect laugh."

"You can't imagine how long it's been since I've felt like laughing. Lately it seems like my life is just this never-ending cycle of . . ."

"Stuff?"

"Yeah."

"I can relate to that," he said, feeling it was safe to open up. "I keep pretty busy with all of my students."

"What about your family?"

"My mother passed away three years ago," he explained.

"Oh, I'm sorry."

"I am, too. She was a difficult woman, but I still miss her keenly. I spent a lot of time trying to figure her out. She was always so bitter, so frustrated. I never really knew why."

"Some people get like that as they age. Life doesn't go the way they expected it to, and they can't seem to gauge their reactions."

"She always took everything to heart. Wore her emotions on her sleeve. Guess that's why it bothers me to see women like that."

"What about your father?" Laura took a bite of her sandwich.

"My dad died when I was in my late teens." Andrew's heart ached with the memory. "He was such an amazing man. He knew everything there was to know about history, about everything."

"Everything?"

Not everything, Andrew had to admit. His father had been very well schooled, had learned much about the world he lived in. But he had never really cared to learn about the things that seemed important to his mother — church, faith, the Bible . . .

Maybe that's why she was so bitter.

"Andrew?" Laura gave him an odd look.

"Oh, I'm sorry. I lost my train of thought. I was just remembering how my dad treated my mom. He didn't care for her religion."

"She was a religious woman?"

"Oh, very."

"What do you mean by religious?"

Andrew shrugged. "She went to church a lot. Took me along for the ride. Like I said, I was a Sunday school kid. She preached at my dad a lot, always tried to get him to go with her. But he wasn't interested. After a few years, I wasn't either. It just seemed like my dad was more exciting. He was so smart, one of the brightest men I ever knew."

"If you don't mind my asking, how did your father . . . I mean, how did he . . ."

"How did he die?" Andrew began to tremble slightly, remembering. He took a deep breath before continuing. "It was a couple of days before my seventeenth birthday. My dad was late coming home from work. My mom got supper ready, as usual, but he just never came. Finally, after a couple of hours, she started making calls. In the middle of all of that, there was a knock at the door — a police officer."

"He'd been in an accident?"

"His car was struck by an eighteen-wheeler," Andrew said, shaking his head. The memory still carried the pain of a seventeen-year-old boy's broken heart. "When my dad died, something in me just sort of gave up, too."

"I can understand that," Laura said softly. "When my husband passed away, I felt like I couldn't go on. He was so much a part of me. Or vice versa. I don't really know how that works, but it hurts so terribly when they're gone."

Andrew looked at her tenderly. "I'm so sorry."

"So your mom was a widow at a young age."

"Yeah, I guess you could say that. She was in her forties when he passed away." Andrew suddenly realized what he was saying and how closely it paralleled Laura's story. "Oh, Laura."

"I think I can understand where some of your mother's bitterness came from. I've struggled with it since Greg died. But last Sunday . . ."

"What about last Sunday?" His curiosity grew.

"Last Sunday, something happened at church. I'm not sure if I can explain it exactly, but God did something in me. He . . . He . . ."

Andrew's heart raced. *Last Sunday. Something was stirring in me, too.*

"I spent some time at the altar Sunday morning after everyone else left the service. I think, for the first time, I was really able to deal with my unforgiveness."

"Unforgiveness?"

"Remember I told you the other day in the chapel that I had been angry? Angry at Greg?"

He nodded.

"I needed to deal with that. It's one thing to carry around anger and frustration. It's another thing to get rid of it, to give it to God."

She makes it sound so easy.

She glanced at her watch, suddenly coming to life. "Oh no. We've been gone nearly thirty minutes. I really need to get back to Kent. He might be waking up, and I want to be there for him." She rose abruptly, wiping crumbs from her blouse.

Andrew stood to join her. "I should probably go, anyway." They stared at each other in silence for a moment before either spoke.

"Thanks for the roses."

His heart leaped as she reached to squeeze his hand. "You're more than welcome," he said, not wanting to let go.

CHAPTER 21

On Thanksgiving morning, Andrew visited the hospital once again.

By now, Laura had grown accustomed to seeing him. He had become as familiar as the flowers from friends at church, which lined the windowsill. However, she hadn't expected him today. *Not on Thanksgiving.*

She stood as he entered the room. "Why are you here?"

"I just had to see for myself. Jess told me he was up walking around this morning."

"Jess? You've talked to Jessica?"

Kent groaned loudly, interrupting them.

"Looks like he's awake, all right."

"I can use all the sympathy I can get." Kent struggled to roll over in the bed. "My arm is killing me." He let out a dramatic moan.

"I'll bet," Andrew said with a laugh. "But this too shall pass. I'm Andrew Dougherty," he said, nodding in Kent's direction.

Laura watched for her son's response. "Kent Chapman." There was an extended pause as he looked Andrew over. "So you're the infamous professor. We meet at last. Thanks for the CD, by the way."

"You're welcome. But I see my fame precedes me."

"Oh yeah." Kent nodded. "I'll say."

"I'm not sure how to take that," Andrew said with a laugh. "So I'll just take it as a compliment."

Kent looked up his mother. "He's not half as bad as you said, Mom. He actually looks like a pretty nice guy."

Laura groaned loudly. "Kent . . ."

"So," Andrew said, looking her in the eye, "what has your mom been saying about me?"

Laura's heart hit the floor. She sent a glaring look Kent's way, but it didn't seem to phase him.

"She says you're tough as nails." Kent looked up at her curiously. "What's that other name you use so much, Mom?"

Laura's gaze shifted to the floor. *Slave driver.* But she couldn't force herself to say it. Why did she suddenly feel like such a heel?

"Hateful?" Andrew guessed, looking at them both.

"Nah. That's not it." Kent shook his head. "It was something else. . . ."

"Prideful?"

Laura looked up on that one. He had been prideful, though she had never said so.

"No," Kent said. "I think it was . . ." He lost himself in his thoughts for a moment before answering. "Slave driver. She said you were a slave driver."

Andrew shook his head, then gave Laura a nod. "Can't argue with that one," he said, almost playfully. "Looks like she hit the nail right on the head."

"Well, anyway," Kent said, "you don't seem like such a bad guy. I don't know what she was talking about."

"Thanks, Kent," Andrew said. "I'm glad someone in here sees me for who I am."

Laura groaned aloud at that one.

"So, what are you doing here, anyway?" Kent's question was blunt, but frankly, Laura had been wondering the same thing. Why did Andrew keep showing up day after day? She looked up at him. Just a few short months ago they had felt so differently about each other and now . . .

Now she didn't know what to think. He had become a regular member of the family.

"I'd do the same for any of my students,"

Andrew said, his eyes looking straight into Laura's. She felt her face flush.

"Sure you would," Kent said.

"Anyway, Jess said to tell you 'hello.' " Andrew reached over to straighten up the flowers in a nearby vase.

"You've seen Jessica today?" Laura asked incredulously. How could that be? Her daughter hadn't been up to the hospital since early morning, and it certainly wasn't a school day.

"Yeah. Well, I took a turkey over to your place before coming here." He spoke the words with a slight tremor in his voice. His focus shifted up to her face.

"You did what?" She couldn't believe it. He had actually been to her house. "How do you know where I live?"

"Oh, well, I . . ."

Ah. Of course. His friend in the registrar's office. *I'll have to remember to report him later.*

"Jess says she wants you to come home and have Thanksgiving dinner with her," Andrew explained. "She misses you."

"I have to stay here. Kent needs me." As much as she would love to go home for a few hours, she simply couldn't. Her conscience wouldn't allow it. How could she leave Kent alone?

"Aw, Mom, I don't need you. I'd feel better if you went home and had Thanksgiving with Grandma and Buck."

"My mother and stepfather are coming over later this afternoon," Laura explained. "In fact, my mom plans to bring a turkey, too, I think."

"Well, there should be plenty for all, then," Andrew said with a laugh. "So why don't you go on home, and I'll stay here with Kent?"

"You would do that? Why?" Why would he make such an offer?

"Sure. Why not?"

She stood for a moment, contemplating his offer. Maybe she could go home for a few hours. Kent didn't seem to mind, and she would love to take a shower and get cleaned up before coming back to the hospital for the night. A Thanksgiving dinner certainly wouldn't hurt either.

"Are . . . are you sure you wouldn't mind?" Laura asked as she looked back and forth between Kent and Andrew.

"I don't mind if he doesn't mind," Andrew said.

"Get out of here, Mom. You deserve a break."

"I won't be gone long. Maybe a couple of hours."

Andrew dropped into a chair. "Take your time. We can play cards, or watch TV, or something."

Laura looked intently at him, hardly recognizing her own voice as she spoke: "Well, maybe you could . . . maybe you could join us for Thanksgiving dinner in about an hour and a half. That is, if Kent doesn't mind staying here alone for a while."

"I told you, Mom, I don't need a sitter. Go home and eat until you're sick. Just bring me some turkey when you're done. And some sweet potatoes."

"You've got a deal." She headed for the door but then turned back, looking at Andrew once again. "An hour and a half?"

"Great," he said, then directed his attention to Kent.

She left the room, headed out into the hallway. It was only when she was about halfway to the car that she realized what she had done. "The professor's coming to my house for dinner."

She thought about him as she made the drive home. She'd grown attached to him over the past few days and had come to rely on his visits. Beyond that, she had learned to enjoy his company, really enjoy it. He was a good man, a kind man.

Is that wrong, Lord? Are my feelings wrong?

She prayed as she drove, trying to come to grips with her changing emotions. By the time she reached the house, she could no longer deny the obvious. "I think I'm falling for this guy." How or why it had happened, she couldn't be sure, but she was sure of one thing. She liked him. A lot.

Laura approached the house with a smile on her face, anxious to see her family. She opened the door and called out, "Is anyone home?"

"We're here, Mom." Jessica exited the kitchen wearing a flour-covered apron.

"What in the world?"

"I'm helping Grandma. We just finished rolling out the homemade biscuits. I mixed them myself." Jessica threw her arms around her, planting a floury kiss on her cheek.

Laura acquired a noseful of the white, powdery stuff and sneezed. "Uh-huh. I can see that. How long till dinner's ready?"

"A little over an hour," Laura's mother said, popping her head out of the kitchen door. "And don't be late."

"That gives me plenty of time for a shower." She headed for her bedroom. "I feel grungy."

"Well, we certainly can't have that at the dinner table. Go take your shower, Mom. We can smell you from here."

Moments later, Laura relaxed under the steady stream of warm water. It felt like heaven. Every time she closed her eyes, she saw herself, head tightly pressed against Andrew's shoulder in the chapel of the hospital. He certainly hadn't seemed to mind. She hadn't either. In fact, she had enjoyed the moment, more than she would have admitted just a few short days ago.

"This is so crazy," she said, leaning against the shower wall. Laura's mind drifted to the smell of his jacket, a brand of cologne she hadn't recognized. Nice. Not too strong, not too light. It suited him.

"Is my heart ready for this, Lord?" she whispered.

The peace that followed suddenly motivated her. Laura reached for the shampoo bottle, pouring a large dollop of the golden liquid into her palm. "The professor's coming to my house, and I'm standing here as nervous as a schoolkid."

Energized, she flew into action.

Andrew nervously knocked at the door. Jessica answered with a shocked look on her face.

"I'm here." He offered up a brave smile.

"You're here," she echoed. "Uh, come on in." She hesitantly opened the door.

Awkwardness kicked in. "Didn't your mom tell you I was coming?"

"She must have forgotten that, but she's been a little preoccupied lately."

"That's understandable."

"Please come on in. I'm sure she'll be out of the shower soon. We're having dinner in about thirty minutes. Are you hungry?"

"Starved."

"Well, have a seat." She gestured to the couch.

He sat reluctantly.

"You the fellow who brought the turkey?" An elderly man entered the room.

Andrew rose, extending his hand.

Jessica made the introductions. "This is my grandfather, Buck Timmons. I'm sure he'll keep you occupied till dinner's done."

"Guess she thinks I've got a big mouth," Buck said, "but that ain't true. I like to talk with the best of 'em, sure, but I know when to quit. What is it you do for a living again, Mr . . . ?"

"Andrew. Andrew Dougherty. I teach at the college. In fact, Jessica and Laura are both in one of my classes."

"Well, I don't know anything about your teaching skills," Buck said as he joined him on the couch, "but you sure know how to pick your turkeys. I just carved your bird, myself."

"I'm glad to finally have an excuse to cook it," Andrew felt the weight lift off of his shoulders. "To be honest, someone gave it to me awhile back, and it's just been taking up room in my freezer. I don't have any family in the area, so I started to think it would stay in there forever."

"No family, eh?" Buck gave him a wink.

"Uh, no, sir."

The elderly man dove headlong into a discussion about the merits of family. Andrew sat quietly, listening as he rambled on and on about every conceivable thing. Their conversation transitioned from families to the battles Buck fought in the Korean War. "You fight in 'Nam, boy?"

"No," Andrew said. "I was just a kid."

"Probably for the best. I tell ya, fighting for your country can be a blessing and a curse all at the same time. Wait. Didn't I hear someone say you taught history?"

"Yes, I teach American History," Andrew said, smiling.

"Well then, if anyone knows your battles, you do."

The older man transitioned into another story about his journey across the Pacific on a battleship as Andrew politely listened. He found himself slightly distracted by the photos of Laura and her husband on the wall across the room. Another smaller snapshot of the whole family sat on the end table next to him. Without thinking, he reached to pick it up and ran his finger over Laura's brown hair.

"That Laura . . . ," Buck exclaimed. "She's a pretty filly, ain't she? I always said she was the spittin' image of her mother. They both just get prettier every day."

Andrew nodded, not sure how to answer. He found himself captivated by the face next to Laura's. This had to be her husband. He had been a handsome man — fair-skinned, with auburn hair and an inviting smile. His eyes glowed with a warmth that spoke of friendship.

"Greg was a great man. Did you ever meet him?"

Andrew shook his head, suddenly apprehensive.

"A great man," Buck repeated with a sigh. "Just about the best father a kid could ever have. And so good to Laura. They were still very much in love, just like young kids. It like to broke her heart when he passed, it really did."

Andrew set the picture back down, not wanting to hear anymore. Suddenly he felt like a stranger in this place, a man who didn't belong. He could never fill the shoes of the man in this picture. Why would he even try to? He stood suddenly, knowing he must leave. He had to back out of this thing before it was too late, before . . .

Laura stuck her head out of the bedroom door, shouting, "Jessica, could you get my jeans out of the dryer?" She had tossed on an old terry-cloth robe and wore a towel around her head but didn't figure her mother or Buck would mind. "Jess?" No answer. Laura stepped out into the living room, hollering a little louder. "Jess!"

"Laura?" She looked up at the sound of Buck's voice to find herself face-to-face with Andrew Dougherty.

"Oh, my goodness!" She clutched at her robe. "I'm — I'm so sorry. I didn't know you were here. You're early." For a moment, Laura felt a familiar frustration rise up within her. Then, just as suddenly, it was replaced with an odd sense of satisfaction that he had come. *I can't let him see me like this.* She backed toward the bedroom.

"Kent fell asleep," Andrew explained, "and the nurse said she didn't see any point in my staying. His medication should keep him out like a light for a couple of hours — at least, that's what she said. I just came on over. I'm sorry. I should probably go."

But I don't want you to. She gave him an imploring look. "No, please don't go. If you'll excuse me, I'll just be a minute." She backed into the bedroom, overcome with embarrassment. "Jess!" she called once more, peeking her head out of the door. She watched as Jessica raced across the living room, a pair of jeans in her hand.

"I'm coming, Mom. I'm coming." She practically knocked the professor down as she passed by him. She entered the bedroom, closing the door behind her.

Laura trembled as she pulled the towel off of her hair. "Help me, Jess," she whispered as she flipped on the blow-dryer and ran a brush through her hair.

"What's wrong with you, Mom? What's got you so shook up?" Jess teased.

"Nothing. Just help me." Laura fought with her brush until her hair was nearly dry. She grabbed her jeans, struggling to slide into them. Her hands shook so hard, she could barely get them up.

"Mom . . ."

"I don't have time, Jess."

"Mom, you're putting your jeans on backwards."

"Oh." She turned them around and tried again.

"Much better," Jessica said. "What'll you wear with them?"

"Get my peach sweater out of the closet." Laura put on a pair of earrings.

"You mean your 'special occasion' peach sweater?"

"It's Thanksgiving, Jessica. That's a special occasion, isn't it?" Her hands still trembled as she fought to put her earrings in.

"What's wrong with you, Mom? You're acting like a giddy schoolgirl with a crush."

"That's crazy." Laura tried to avoid looking her daughter in the eye. Why was it so hard to admit she actually liked this man? *I do like him, very much. More than I could admit to Jess or anyone else.*

She quickly applied some lipstick and blush, then ran the brush through her hair one last time. "Do I look okay?" she asked, turning for Jess's approval.

"You look great, Mom. Now get out there and knock him dead." Jessica clapped her hand over her mouth, realizing what she had said. "I'm so sorry. I didn't mean . . ."

Laura grinned a silly grin. "It's okay. It's about time we got back to joking around here. You just be yourself, and everything will be fine."

Andrew tried to compose himself as Laura

entered the room. Keeping his emotions in check proved to be very difficult. Her hair was still slightly damp, but it carried the familiar aroma of flowers. She wore the same sweater she had worn at the game — the one he remembered so well. She completely took his breath away.

"I hope you didn't mind waiting." Laura looked as nervous as he felt. "I just had to change before going back up to the hospital. You understand."

Of course he understood. He would have understood if she had decided to paper and paint the living room before going back.

"Everything smells great, Mom." Laura gave her mother a hug. "Professor Dougherty, have you met my mother, Violet Timmons?"

"Just call me Vi," the older woman responded.

He shook Violet's hand firmly and smiled, knowing from her easygoing smile she would be easy to like.

"Well, why don't we all go on into the dining room," Vi said, leading the way, "before everything gets cold."

Laura watched Andrew carefully as he made his way into the dining room. Buck pulled out the seat that had always been Greg's and gestured for Andrew to sit down. Immediately, Laura's heart began to twist inside her. *Greg's chair. No one else should sit there. No one. Not yet, anyway.* She reluctantly sat across from Andrew, unable to focus.

"Let's pray, shall we?" Buck said with a smile as he looked around the table.

Laura glanced in Andrew's direction, trying to read his reaction. How would he feel about this? Would he be offended, or . . . She was relieved to see that he bowed his head reverently and closed his eyes. She did the same. Buck began to pray a deep, genuine prayer, thanking God for Kent's recovery and for the food provided. He added a special prayer of thanks for Andrew's gift of the turkey, but Laura barely heard it. Her eyes were once again fixed on Greg's chair.

Heads lifted, and the food began to make its way around the table. Everyone chatted and laughed as if nothing in the world could be wrong. But something felt wrong, very wrong.

"Laura, honey, would you pass the potatoes?" She numbly passed them to her mother, trying to focus.

"I'll have the dressing, Laura," Buck said, reaching out for it. She nodded but never touched it, her focus drifting once again to the chair.

"Mom, are you okay?" Jessica asked, looking at her curiously.

"Oh. Yeah, sure." *I'm not.* A war had suddenly and inexplicably risen up inside of her. There was no logical reason why she should feel this sudden anger, but she couldn't seem to stop it.

"I'll take a roll," Andrew said, looking directly at her with a smile. She picked up the basket, clutching it tightly. She couldn't seem to release it.

"Mom?" Jessica gazed at her with a worried expression.

"Oh, I —" She passed the rolls without further explanation, turning her attention to her own plate. She could do this. She wouldn't humiliate herself or anyone else. Not today, not when everything was so perfect. She looked up again, and a very clear picture of Greg seated in the chair greeted her. Suddenly, Laura could take it no more. "I — I have to get out of here," she said, standing.

"What do you mean?" her mother asked.

"I — I have to get back to the hospital. I'm sure you all understand. Kent needs me."

Andrew stood immediately. "Maybe I

should leave. It's getting late, anyway."

"No, please don't go, Mr. Dougherty," Buck said. "You're our guest. You just sit right down and eat."

"Really," Laura said, trying not to look at him. "Just because I'm leaving doesn't mean you have to." She practically ran to the front door, throwing it open. "If anyone needs me, I'll be at the hospital."

She stepped outside into the cool autumn air and leaned back against the house, where her tears flowed freely.

Andrew stood up from the table, excusing himself. He needed to catch up with Laura before she left. He had so much to say to her. She couldn't just slip away — not this time. He had lost her this way before, and he wasn't about to let it happen again.

He opened the front door, expecting to find her in her car, but she was propped up against the side of the house, sobbing.

"Laura?"

She looked at him fearfully. "I'm — I'm sorry. I have to go."

He reached out to take her arm, but she eluded him. "Laura, please wait. I need to talk to you."

"I can't talk to you right now, Andrew." She moved away from him.

"I just want to tell you something. Please." He felt like his heart would burst if he didn't say it.

"Can't it wait?" she asked impatiently.

"No, it can't. I can't." His ears were ringing now. *Just get through this.*

"What's so important?" She took a few steps toward her car, obviously trying to avoid him. He followed her closely.

"You remember that conversation we had in the hospital cafeteria yesterday?" he asked breathlessly. "Something really, I don't know . . . amazing happened to me when I got home last night. For the first time in years, I found myself able to pray."

She looked up at him with tears in her eyes. "Really?"

"Yes. I asked God to forgive me for being so angry with Him. That happened because of you, Laura." He reached to take her hand. She let him hold it for a moment, then pulled away. "Don't you see? I would never have had the courage to face the truth if it hadn't been for you."

"The truth . . . ," she stammered. "It's the truth that's killing me right now. The truth of how I felt about Greg. The truth about how scared I am when I see someone else sitting in his chair."

"So that's what it is."

"Yes." Tears filled her beautiful eyes again.

Andrew reached out to brush them away, but she pushed his hand away. "Can't we at least talk about this?" he implored. "Please?"

"Maybe someday," she said as she pulled the car door open.

"When?"

"I don't know," she spoke through the emotion. "I just can't right now. I can't." She jumped into her car and sped away, leaving his heart in a state of chaos. With his head hanging, Andrew climbed into his car and drove away.

CHAPTER 22

"Mom, it's been two weeks, and you haven't even spoken a word to him. That's not fair."

Laura did her best to ignore her daughter. Frustration overwhelmed her these days. She seemed to always be in a bad mood at home. She had thrown herself into her work with a vengeance. "I don't expect you to understand, Jessica," she said finally. "I'm just confused, that's all. I need time. Space."

"Confused about him?"

"Him who?"

"You know who, Mom. The professor. The one you've been avoiding for the last two weeks."

"I haven't been avoiding him," Laura argued. "I've been going to class, haven't I?"

"Yes, but you haven't said a word to him," Jessica commented. "Everyone's noticed. The whole class is talking about it."

"The whole class?"

"Yes."

"What are they saying?"

"They're just wondering what's up. The kids loved the bickering that went on between the two of you, and now it's just nothing but silence. It's boring. You're boring."

"Thanks a lot."

"No, I mean it, Mom. You've got to snap out of this. Whatever he's done, you need to forgive him. Remember, we talked about that. Forgiveness is everything."

"It's nothing he's done, Jessica. That's the problem."

"What do you mean?"

"I mean . . . ," Laura hesitated. "I mean, he's not your father. He never will be. There will never be another man like your dad." Surely Jessica would understand.

Her daughter looked her squarely in the eye. "You're right, Mom. He's not Daddy. But did you ever consider the fact that God might be bringing you something — someone — completely different?"

"He's different, all right." Laura smiled.

"Maybe you shouldn't be looking for someone like Daddy at all. Maybe you should just be open to any man God might bring into your life, no matter how different he is."

244

"What?" Laura was stunned at her daughter's tenacity.

"No one can ever take Daddy's place — that's true. But you don't have to worry that we'll forget him, Mom. He's always here, in my heart." Jessica's voice trembled with emotion as she continued. "But you've got things all confused where the professor's concerned. Maybe all he needs to do is just be himself."

"You're right, Jess. I know you are," Laura said softly.

But what could she do? There were too many bridges crossed, too many things left undone.

Three weeks and counting. Andrew paced around his classroom, tormented by the struggle that ensued in his heart and his head. His head convinced him he should give up — not pursue any type of relationship with Laura Chapman, friendship or otherwise. His heart cried out for more, much more. As the semester came to a close, he faced an inevitable deadline. Grades for American History had just been averaged. Laura's good, solid A had been earned without any assistance from him. She had aced his class. Not many people could boast of that.

Of course, it might not have happened if Dick DeHart hadn't gotten involved. Andrew's skin began to crawl. The idea of any other man looking at Laura — his Laura — made him so angry, he could hardly see straight. *But she's not my Laura. She doesn't want to be with me. She made that abundantly clear on Thanksgiving.* It had started . . . when had it started, again? *Ah yes. When I sat in that chair.* A light tap on the door distracted him. He looked up, shocked to see Jessica standing there with a concerned look on her face.

"Professor Dougherty," she said hesitantly. "Can I come in?"

"Sure, Jess. What's up?"

She looked a little nervous. "I just wanted to talk to you. Of course, my mom would kill me if she knew I came."

"What do you mean?"

"I mean," she said, "I think you need to know that she's, she's just . . ."

"Just what?" He waited anxiously to hear the rest of the sentence.

"Scared," Jessica said finally. "She's scared to death."

He dropped into a chair, his forehead breaking out in a sweat.

"You don't look like you're in much better shape than she is," Jessica said with a

246

laugh. "This is really pathetic."

"I'm not very good at this."

"I'll say. That's why I'm here to help you."

"Help me?" *She's just a kid. How can she help me?*

"Yep. My mom's at the Bookstop, and I want you to go there to see her."

"She's back at work?"

"Has been for a week and a half. Kent's back in school and doing great," she explained.

"That's good."

"Yeah. Well, anyway, she's back at work; but her mind isn't on her work, I'll tell you that much."

"It's not?"

"No, it's not."

"If you don't mind my asking —" he stammered.

"She can't stop thinking about you," Jessica explained. "I know because she talks about you all of the time. She's scared of how she feels, that's all."

"I can relate to that." Andrew looked at the ground. "I'm pretty, well, I mean — I'm a little scared, too."

"You two are like a couple of kids," Jessica said finally. "But don't you worry. Just leave everything up to me."

Andrew's heart beat so fast, he could

barely breathe. "Are you sure about this?"

"More than sure," Jessica said.

He suddenly knew what he had to do. He would go to her. Somehow, someway he would communicate his love for her in a way that wouldn't threaten the memory of her husband. He could do that. With the Lord's help, he could do that.

"Can I ask you a personal question?" Jessica looked him in the eye.

"Sure. Why not?" Everything he had ever kept hidden had already come out over the past few days.

"Do you pray, Professor Dougherty?"

He paused before answering. "If you had asked me that question a few weeks ago, I would have answered so differently. But I do pray, Jessica. Believe it or not, I've been spending a lot of time in prayer over the past few weeks." He had felt years of coldness toward the Lord melt away in the process.

"Well then, if you want to see those prayers answered, get on over there to the bookstore and tell my mom how you feel. If she's half the woman I know she is, she won't break your heart. At least, I don't think she will."

The words "at least" nearly drove a stake through Andrew's fragile heart, and yet they propelled him to his feet. "I'll do it," he said, suddenly energized. "It may seem crazy, but I'll do the impossible."

"Professor," Jessica called out to him as he bolted through the door. He turned and looked at her one last time.

"Yes?"

" 'With God all things are possible.' "

" 'With God all things are possible.' " He repeated the words, feeling the smile return to his face. "Thanks, Jessica. Thanks for everything."

"Hey," she hollered, as he sprinted down the hallway toward the parking lot. "Does this mean I get an A in your class?"

Andrew didn't answer. After all, he didn't want to spoil what had suddenly become a perfect moment.

Laura passed through the inspirational section of the bookstore, taking another look at the book that had long captivated her attentions: *Put Your Troubles in the Blender and Give Them a Spin*. She stood in silence, thumbing through the book. Funny in some places, it struck a serious nerve in others. Many of the situations in the book were not unlike her own. Somehow this author, also a woman, had triumphed over her tragedies and turned them into victories using humor.

"It should be so simple," Laura mumbled as she placed the book on the shelf. "So, what do you think, Madeline?" She turned to look at her friend. "Do you think I should or I shouldn't?"

"Should or shouldn't what?" the woman asked.

"Should I or shouldn't I . . ." Laura's heart beat so hard, it took her breath away. It had been many, many years since talking about a man had made her this nervous. "Take a chance," Laura stammered finally. "With the professor." She looked nervously at Madeline. What she found there was warmth and understanding.

"I've been hoping for quite some time that you would find someone."

"Really?"

"Yep."

"I wasn't even praying for this," Laura said with a sigh.

"Don't you see?" Madeline interjected. "That's exactly what makes it so special. God knew what you needed and wanted even before you did. Besides, it's about time you had a fella in your life. To be honest, I had hoped my brother would be the one, but . . ."

"I'm so sorry, Madeline, but Dick just wasn't my type." She said the words firmly.

Perhaps a little too firmly.

"I know. He's a Romeo, that's for sure," Madeline responded. "It may make you feel better to know he's already dating someone from the university."

"Good grief." Somehow knowing that did make her feel a little better.

"So do you think I should go up to the school and see Andrew?" Laura asked. "He's probably still there. I think so, anyway."

"I wouldn't waste another minute. You get in that car of yours and make haste all the way down to the college. Go. Don't worry about the shop. I'm here."

"Are you sure?" Laura's heart raced, making it difficult to breathe.

"Completely sure," Madeline said. "Get out of here."

Laura sprinted to the door. "See you later, Madeline." She raced toward the car, turning the key in the ignition. *I can't believe I'm doing this! I'm actually going to tell him how I feel.*

Andrew drove like a maniac along the interstate, fighting traffic all the way. "Come on . . . ," he grumbled at the cars in front of him. They crawled along, ignoring his pleas. "Just a couple of miles. It's not that far."

251

He had already decided what he would say. He would tell her exactly what he felt, what his intentions were. If she rejected him this time, he would give up. Plain and simple. Andrew reached the exit for Tully, pulling off onto the feeder road. In just a couple of minutes he would see her.

He would tell her.

CHAPTER 23

"Is Laura here?" Andrew asked, his eyes bearing down on Madeline's.

"Oh, dear. Oh, dear," she said, looking as nervous as a cat. "I'm so sorry."

"She's not here? Where did she go?"

"Well, actually, she went to the college to try to find you," Madeline explained.

"To find me? Why?" *This is too confusing.*

"She wanted to . . . ," Madeline stammered. "She was going to . . . It's like this . . ."

"Could you please just say it?" Andrew hollered, feeling his face go hot.

Madeline stood frozen, saying nothing.

"Fine," he said, turning toward the door. "You say she's at the school? I'm going back to the school." Andrew groaned loudly as he headed back to his car.

Laura paced back and forth in the empty

classroom, her heart feeling as if it would break.

"Where is he?" The door stood wide open. He never left it open unless he happened to be nearby, but he didn't appear to be anywhere.

She plopped down onto the edge of his desk, deep in thought. Her eyes traveled the familiar room, drinking in the things that Andrew loved. American history. She had somehow managed to make it through his course with flying colors, with or without assistance from Dick DeHart. If nothing else, she could be very proud of that.

But something else captivated her mind, something that wouldn't rest. She had to talk to Andrew, had to tell him how she felt. She did have feelings for him, she had to admit — strong feelings. Her conversation with Jessica had convinced her of that. God had arranged all of this. But she had treated Andrew so badly on Thanksgiving. Would he forgive her?

Laura's thoughts shifted, wandering back to the day when she had walked in on him in this very room — a day when a dark-haired woman sat in the very spot she found herself. Was it possible? Was Andrew involved with her, the girl from the cafeteria? They had been seen together on more than one occasion, deep in conversation.

And yet Andrew had swept her into his arms with such tenderness that day in the chapel. The look in his eyes spoke of more than friendship.

Laura stood and walked across the room toward the door. She gave the walls one last glance as she left, running her finger across the Declaration of Independence. She pulled the door shut behind her, realizing it could very well be the last time she would ever step inside this room.

Andrew raced back out to his car, immediately climbing inside. "Please be there," he whispered as he turned the key in the ignition. So many unanswered questions lingered in his mind. *Why did she go back to the school? Is it possible . . . ?*

Moments later, he entered the interstate, accelerating much faster than usual up the entrance ramp. He raced along, honking his horn at any driver who had the nerve to drive the speed limit. Finally he arrived at the school. Anxiously, he turned into the parking lot.

He raced from the car to the history classroom. *Please be here.* He made his way up the hallway, quickly opening the door to his classroom. *Empty.* Andrew made his way to his desk, dropping into the chair. He buried his head in his hands. "This is too much. I can't do this anymore."

"Well, what happened?" Jessica appeared at the door.

"She wasn't there. Madeline said she was on her way here. Have you seen her?"

"Nope. I've been waiting in the cafeteria with my nose buried in a book. I had a feeling you'd come back here afterward."

He sighed deeply. "This is such a mess."

Jessica plopped down in a chair, staring up at him. "I'm really sorry about all of this."

"It's okay. I should probably just go home and sleep it off. Maybe I can try again tomorrow."

"Well," Jessica said, "I have this one little problem."

"What?"

"I need a ride home. You don't really mind, do you?"

Mind? Of course he didn't mind. He lived for days like this. "Come on," he said, reaching for his keys once again. "Let's get out of here."

Laura climbed into the shower, talking to herself. "What's wrong with me?" she mumbled. She allowed the water to run over her hair to cool her down. "Andrew Dougherty probably thinks I'm the biggest flake on the planet."

She pulled out her favorite shampoo, working it into lather. Scrubbing her head vigorously, she continued the conversation with herself. "I'm crazy to think I need a guy in my life. I don't need anyone. I don't."

She leaned against the shower wall, tears cascading down her face. Her heart began to beat so hard, she could barely breathe.

"I may not need him," she whispered to herself. "But I love him."

She stepped out of the shower, agitated. "Of course he wasn't at the school," she grumbled. "Why should he be at the school just because he teaches there?" She wrapped herself in her bathrobe, still upset. "Where else would he be? He probably doesn't want to talk to me, anyway."

Frustrated, she pulled a towel up around her wet hair and looked in the mirror. "It's not like I'm pretty," she said, staring at her reflection. "I'm not even close to pretty." What Greg had seen in her, she had never understood. A solemn reflection met her gaze — an ever-present reminder of the fact that she was average, ordinary.

Laura reached up into the medicine chest and pulled out a container. "Not that this will do much good." She smeared the gooey mask all over her face. When she finished, the only things left visible were her mouth and eyes. "Anyway, it's not like he's such a great catch," she reasoned with herself. "He doesn't even know how to dress. His clothes are wrinkled, and his ties are older than my children. He's as hopeless as I am."

Laura made her way across the bedroom, still talking to herself. Somehow, it made her feel better. "And his hair," she continued. "It wouldn't hurt the man to use some hair gel. It wouldn't wound his ego that much, would it?"

Frustrated, she pulled the bedroom door open, feeling the mask begin to harden. A cup of hot chocolate would make everything better. It always did.

"Men," she exclaimed, stepping out into the living room. "They don't know what they're missing, anyway."

"Mom?"

"Yeah?" She didn't even look up, still lost in her private conversation.

"Uh, Mom?"

"What, Jessica?" she asked, exasperated.

"I just thought you might want to know we have company."

Laura turned abruptly, finding herself face-to-face with Professor Andrew Dougherty. Her heart leaped into her throat. Suddenly she wasn't sure whether to throw her arms around him or to turn and run.

Andrew took one look at Laura and started laughing. He couldn't seem to control himself. Whether the laughter came from the sheer relief of finding her at last, or the fact that her face was covered in the thick green mask, he couldn't be sure. How comical, yet how endearing. He had never seen anything like it on any woman, let alone the one he now found himself helplessly, hopelessly in love with. "Laura?" It was more question than statement.

She instinctively put her hands up over her face, clearly embarrassed. "Oh, no . . . Not now. Not like this!"

"Please don't hide your face," he said, reaching for her hands. "It's beautiful." His hands trembled uncontrollably as they clutched hers.

"You're making fun of me," she pouted, backing toward the bedroom.

Andrew's heart pounded loudly in his ears, which were heating up more with each passing moment. He could hardly breathe, let alone think or speak like a rational man. "Laura, the last thing on earth I want to do is make fun of you. I think you're beautiful

— green face and all."

"You do?"

"I do." He spoke the words almost pro-phetically. There would be no more broken hearts in his world. He had waited for Laura Chapman all of his life, and she was well worth the wait.

She continued to take tiny, nervous steps backward until she ran smack-dab into the living room wall. Jessica stood off to one side of the room, giggling helplessly.

Kent stuck his head in from the kitchen, his jaw dropping. "Mom?" He looked more than a little surprised.

"Kent," Andrew said, turning toward him, "your mother and I are having a little conversation. You don't mind, do you?"

"Not a bit," Kent said, heading back into the kitchen.

"Jessica," Andrew said firmly, turning to look at her. "I think your brother needs your help in the kitchen." He gave her a look that could not be misunderstood.

"Whatever you say," Jessica agreed. "You're the teacher."

Laura looked up into the sparkling eyes of this man who had captivated her. How clear everything suddenly seemed.

"I feel like I've known you forever, not

just a few months," he said as he reached to touch her crusty cheek.

Months? It seemed she had always known Andrew, always felt drawn to him as she did now. It was true that he could never take Greg's place. But, then again, maybe he wasn't supposed to. Maybe, like Jessica said, he only needed to be himself.

But how could she begin to break through the layers of unspoken words that had traveled between them over the last several weeks? Laura had rehearsed the prepared speech in her head so many times. She would tell him how she felt, what her heart had been longing to say. And yet, no words seemed to come at all. She found herself completely and utterly speechless. Part of that, she had to admit, came from the fact that the mud mask had completely hardened, leaving her with little or no facial movement.

"Ms. Chapman," Andrew said, moving closer to her. She looked up into his eyes. They were kind eyes, loving eyes. They seemed to reach into the very depths of her soul and touch a spot that had not been touched for a long, long time. For the first time, she saw herself in their reflection. It was wonderful, amazing.

"Yes, Professor Dougherty?" She fought

to form words through tightened lips. The "professor" part was just for emphasis, but it seemed to work like a charm. A grin spread across his face. *I love this man. I love him!* She struggled to catch her breath with the reality of the thought.

"Your very wise daughter asked me today if I was a praying man."

"What did you tell her?" Laura spoke slowly, forcing the words.

"I told her that I was," he answered. "I've taken to praying quite a bit these past three weeks."

"You have?" She tried to smile, but her cheeks refused to cooperate.

"I have, and I can say I'm a firm believer in the power of prayer." A look of determination filled his eyes — a fiery look.

"Really? Is that what you came to tell me?" she asked, half-teasing.

"I came to tell you that you aced my class." He moved closer still.

"I did?" She asked breathlessly, cradling her head in his hand. "I got an A?"

"You got an A," he said, coming so close that her heart began to race. "But that's not the only reason I came."

"It isn't?" Her knees suddenly grew weak, and she felt a little wobbly. The only thing that kept her standing was the wall itself, which she had firmly pressed herself up against.

"Nope," he said, slipping both arms around her neck and pulling her to himself. How right it felt to be in his arms, how totally and perfectly right. "I came to tell you, Ms. Chapman, that, no matter how many students I have, you're absolutely in a class of your own." His breath lingered warm against her lips.

She looked up at him, wanting like crazy to smile, but unable to with her face frozen in position by the mask. "Does that make me the teacher's pet?" she whispered, feeling her heart about to break wide open with the joy that consumed it.

Andrew never took the time to answer. His lips spoke more than words could ever say.

Chapter 24

Laura glanced in the full-length mirror, then turned to look at Madeline. "What do you think?" she asked, as she fussed with her hair.

"What do I think? What do I think?" Madeline's face lit into a broad smile. "I think you're the prettiest bride I've ever seen."

"Exaggeration doesn't suit you," Laura said with a sigh, "but I appreciate the effort."

"I wasn't exaggerating, thank you very much," Madeline said with a smirk. "I meant every word."

After another glance in the mirror, Laura attempted to tame a loose hair, but her trembling hands wouldn't allow it.

"Need help with that?" Madeline gave her a sympathetic look.

"Y–yes." Laura chuckled nervously, then looked in the direction of the door as she heard a knock.

"Mom, are you almost ready?" Jessica's voice rang out.

"Yes, come on in." Laura looked up as her daughter entered the tiny room the church secretary had designated the "Bride's Chambers."

Jessica took one look at her and her eyes filled with tears. "Mom, I always pictured this the other way around. You would be helping *me* dress for *my* wedding. *I'd* be the one in the wedding dress."

"It's not exactly a wedding dress." Laura twirled around to show off the ivory lace dress she had selected for this special day.

"It's a wedding dress all right," Jessica said. "And Andrew's eyes are going to pop when he sees you in it."

"You think?" Laura felt her cheeks flush.

"I think."

Another knock on the door interrupted their conversation. Laura's mother popped her head in the door and began to cry as soon as she saw her daughter. She stepped inside the tiny room and reached inside her purse for a tissue. After just a few seconds, she managed a few words. "I don't think I cried this much at your first wedding." Immediately she clamped a hand over her mouth, as if she'd said something wrong.

Laura took a couple of steps in her direction and offered up a reassuring nod. "It's okay, Mom. I don't mind. And you're right . . . you didn't cry this much at my first wedding."

"I'm just so happy for you, is all," her mother said as she wiped her eyes. "We all are."

Jessica and Madeline nodded their agreement, and all of the women entered into a group hug. For a minute, Laura couldn't speak. She thought about all of the pain she'd felt for so long, the fear. How loneliness had gripped her. And now . . . why, now she could practically soar, she felt so happy. *You've resurrected me, Lord. You've done the impossible.*

Just then, another knock sounded at the door. "Is it okay to come in?" Kent's voice sounded muffled from the other side.

"Come in," Laura called.

When Kent entered the room in his tuxedo, everyone gasped.

"You're a . . . a . . . a man!" His grandmother swept him into her arms.

"A man who reminds me a lot of his father." Laura couldn't help but make the observation. Standing there in his tuxedo, Kent looked for all the world like Greg. A very young Greg, of course, but what a likeness!

"Hey, this day is supposed to be about you." Kent took his mother's hand and gave it a squeeze. "And I happen to know that Andrew is having a fit waiting for you."

"He is?" Laura's cheeks warmed at the thought of it.

"He is." Kent extended his arm. "So let's get this show on the road. The guests are all seated."

Laura drew in a deep breath.

"You can do this, Mom," Jessica whispered. "You'll be just fine."

They left the tiny dressing room together and headed out into the foyer of the church, where they were met by Buck, who gave a little whistle. Even from here, Laura could hear music playing from inside the sanctuary.

Madeline switched into wedding planning gear and started giving instructions. "Okay, mother of the bride, you're first."

Laura watched with a smile as Buck took her mother by the arm and ushered her through the doors into the sanctuary.

The music changed, signaling time for the bridesmaids to enter. Madeline led the way, followed by Jessica.

"Looks like it's just you and me, Mom." Kent gave her a wink, and her heart flip-flopped.

"R–right." She attempted to swallow the lump in her throat, but found it difficult.

As the music for the bridal march filled the auditorium, Kent took her by the arm and they began the long walk down the aisle. Even from here, she could see the tears in Andrew's eyes and noticed the tremor in his hands. *Thank goodness! He's as nervous as I am!*

Maybe nervous wasn't the right word. Overwhelmed? Overjoyed? Yes, that was surely it. She felt overjoyed. So much joy spilled over, there seemed to be no place to contain it.

After what felt like the longest walk in history, Laura reached her husband-to-be. The pastor cleared his throat, then posed the familiar question: "Who gives this woman to be wed to this man?"

Kent's voice shook as he responded, "My sister and I do."

At this point, Kent moved to the front to join Andrew as his best man.

Everything after that was a blur. A joyous, nerve-wracking, blissful blur. Vows. A beautiful solo, sung by Jessica. Exchanging of rings. The kiss . . .

Ah, the kiss! In that moment, as heaven and earth seemed to touch, Laura Chapman . . . no, Laura *Dougherty* . . . found herself wrapped in the arms of the man who would walk with her — arm in arm — through the next season of her life.

Funny. Knowing that almost made all of those ridiculous pop quizzes worthwhile.

EPILOGUE

Laura sat alongside her fellow students, anxiously waiting her turn. Any moment now, she would hear her name. She glanced across the large auditorium to where her family sat in the stands. Kent waved frantically, his new girlfriend, Bridget, joining in. They had only been dating a few weeks, but Laura loved her like a daughter. She was a strong Christian and had made quite an impact in Kent's life. In fact, just this morning Laura had heard the two of them discussing plans to work in the youth ministry at church. *God is so good.*

Her eyes traveled to her mom and Jessica, who sat at their right. As usual, Buck was nearby, a broad grin on his face. They smiled and waved, and Laura's heart began to race in anticipation of what was about to take place.

She glanced to and fro, looking for Andrew. *Ah. There he is, seated just behind them, with a fistful of yellow roses. I'm so glad he's here. He's my biggest fan.* She grinned at them all, waving madly. He blew her a kiss in response. She pretended to catch it, nearly knocking the cap off of the boy sitting next to her.

"So sorry."

"No problem."

Laura turned her attention back to the speaker at the podium, trying to concentrate. He spoke of hope, of potential, of possibilities. They were words she fully understood. In fact, she appreciated them now more than ever.

Laura's two years at Wainesworth Junior College had paid off and then some. With her associate's degree in hand, she had transferred to the university a couple of years back. She would cross the stage to accept her bachelor's degree in Business Management any moment now.

The whole thing had been her husband's idea, really. Laura looked up at Andrew once again, a smile instinctively spreading across her face. His sport jacket and tie were terribly mismatched, and his rumpled hair desperately needed combing. Not much had changed over the years.

She hoped it never would.

The employees of Thorndike Press hope you have enjoyed this Large Print book. All our Thorndike and Wheeler Large Print titles are designed for easy reading, and all our books are made to last. Other Thorndike Press Large Print books are available at your library, through selected bookstores, or directly from us.

For information about titles, please call:
(800) 223-1244

or visit our Web site at:
http://gale.cengage.com/thorndike

To share your comments, please write:
Publisher
Thorndike Press
295 Kennedy Memorial Drive
Waterville, ME 04901